214

P9-ECL-692

BOY
ON THE
EDGE

BOY
ON THE
EDGE

Fridrik Erlings

CANDLEWICK PRESS

This is a work of fiction. Names, characters, places, and incidents are either products of the author's imagination or, if real, are used fictitiously.

Copyright © 2012 by Fridrik Erlings
Published by arrangement with Meadowside Children's Books

Published with the support of Bókmenntasjóður / Icelandic Literature Fund

All rights reserved. No part of this book may be reproduced, transmitted, or stored in an information retrieval system in any form or by any means, graphic, electronic, or mechanical, including photocopying, taping, and recording, without prior written permission from the publisher.

First U.S. edition 2014

Library of Congress Catalog Card Number 2013943072
ISBN 978-0-7636-6680-4

13 14 15 16 17 18 BVG 10 9 8 7 6 5 4 3 2 1

Printed in Berryville, VA, U.S.A.

This book was typeset in ITC Stone Serif.

Candlewick Press
99 Dover Street
Somerville, Massachusetts 02144

visit us at www.candlewick.com

To Simon and Lucy

*Your tireless support and your generous
friendship have turned my hopes
into reality, my fears into courage,
and given me a new language.*

I am with you always,
even unto the end of the world.

(Matthew 28:20)

Prologue

I didn't know that I would ever tell this story. Not because I thought people wouldn't be interested in reading it, but because it was too close to my heart to write it. The years went by and the distance between the memories and myself grew wider, until they had at last all but vanished.

I hadn't visited my native country for almost two decades. I had immersed myself in work, moving from one university to the next, giving lectures, studying, writing books, becoming known in a small circle of history professors, sometimes even appearing on television, talking about Emperor Henry IV and the Investiture Controversy, William the Conqueror, Richard the Lionheart or Charlemagne and the Saxon Wars. I knew everything about them that there was to know. They were my closest friends. That's how lost and lonely I was. My closest companions in life were people long since dead and gone.

I had but one real friend, who wrote me several letters every year. They were always addressed to the university where I had begun my studies, and the office took great care to find my new location and send them onward. After a while I stopped reading them, and placed them unopened in a drawer.

His letters stirred up the guilt I was trying so hard to forget, guilt for moving away. His handwriting, the large clumsy letters, written with a crude pencil, were curiously connected to his voice somehow, so I could almost hear the deep growl in his throat while reading them.

And I never wrote back. What was I to write? I didn't understand what he was telling me, or why: the letters were like solitary pieces of a puzzle, abstract and disconnected.

Strangely enough, his name was Henry William Richard Charles: he was the very namesake of my dead friends, the ancient heroes I admired so much. But the truth is that he was a greater hero than any of them, although I hadn't realized that at the time. He was noble, brave, and loyal.

I spoke my native language, Icelandic, but once a year, when I called Emily, our foster mother. Her tender voice made me feel like the little boy I once was. Cuddled in her warm embrace, I'd felt secure from all the evils of this world. She always asked if I wanted to have a word or two with Henry. But I always replied: Not now, I'll call again soon. But I never did.

I thought he would always be there, just as he always had been.

I had become an empty shell in the present, desperately seeking fulfillment in the long-gone, past stories of dead heroes. But fate had decided to give me one last chance to save my life; or rather Henry came to my rescue. His final heroic deed was to tell me a truly fulfilling story: our own.

I received a message from Emily informing me that Henry

had passed away in his sleep. The funeral would take place in a week's time.

I canceled everything and took a plane home to Iceland.

The funeral was held in a small country church, close to the farm where he and Emily lived, the farm she had bought when the three of us had become a family. It was a solemn ritual, simple and to the point, just as Henry would have liked it. It was the first time I met his mother. She was in a wheelchair, crumbling with age, and the young nurse who accompanied her told me she hadn't spoken a word for more than fifteen years. I squeezed her hand lightly: she didn't react. But when the coffin sank slowly into the grave she moved her hand to wipe away the tears. She must have remembered the little child she'd once held in her arms, before the cruel world tore their lives apart.

It was early spring, Henry's favorite time of the year. I stayed with Emily the whole summer, helping her out during lambing season, milking the cows and then herding them, mowing the field on the old tractor, like Henry and I used to do before I moved away. I had forgotten how the Icelandic summer is like a never-ending day, for at night the sun barely goes below the horizon. It's a very different world from the dark and cold winter months; it's a world full of hope and ethereal beauty. I rode Henry's graceful mare in the bright summer night, following the river to the ocean, and then along the beach that stretched far into the distance.

Henry's room was the same as it had always been, except

for one thing: it was full of books. There were stacks on the floor, and every shelf was crammed right up to the ceiling. There was a double row of books on the windowsill, and twice as many on the table. Under his bed were more boxes full of books. It was like entering a tiny library or a monk's cell, fortified with the finest literature in the world.

Emily smiled when she saw my wonder. "Henry loved to read," she said. Then she patted me on the shoulder and added, "All thanks to you."

I didn't know what she meant by that. "I believe he told you the story in one of his letters," she said.

"When? Which one?" I asked, trying to hide my guilt over the unopened letters. "Some might have gone astray," I tried to explain. "I've been moving a lot, you know."

Then Emily showed me a box full of black notebooks. They were Henry's. He had written a little every day, Emily told me, drafting his letters to me by filling each book with his thoughts and memories, working hard to find the right words to describe his feelings, pouring his heart out, page after page. I felt ashamed for having left so many of his letters unopened. But whatever he had wanted to tell me I would now find in the notebooks.

Autumn came and I began to read, trying to get to know my friend Henry William Richard Charles, my only brother in the world. And reading, I began to put the pieces of the puzzle together, to know and understand. I heard to his deep growling voice whispering to me through his clumsy handwriting and memories started flowing, bursting forth in my mind like vivid scenes in a movie, some bright and happy, others dark and fearful.

Henry had lovingly preserved the past, not for himself, but for me.

Once I finished reading all of his notebooks, my heart knew what to do. It was not a decision made in my mind, not something I brooded over for a long time before I came to a conclusion. It was just something I knew I had to do, not for any reward, not for myself or anyone else, but for Henry alone. I would write his story.

I knew I would have to stay in my home country, gather more information, search through the files of all the institutions, as well as the files of the police. Emily was happy that I had decided to stay, and we had long talks during the dark winter nights that followed. She told me about her past and I began, at last, to untangle the strange web of events that had brought the three of us together all those years ago.

My research revealed more than I could have imagined: newspaper clippings, reports, and the like, but also some unexpected pieces of information, especially when I traveled through the bleak countryside where the Home of Lesser Brethren had once stood in the midst of the lava field. The people in the district were more than willing to tell their stories about the home, where troubled boys from the city were sent. The home run by the neurotic Reverend Oswald and his charming wife, Emily. A home on the edge of the world, where the massive cliffs at Lands End were battered relentlessly by the furious waves of the North Atlantic.

The information gave me a good overview of the period, as well as the background for many of the things that happened. But the bulk and the heart of the story come from Henry. All I've done, really, is put everything together in a continuous narrative.

Henry would never have dreamed that anyone would find his life worthy of becoming a story in a book; on a shelf in a "proper home" read by "proper people," as he would have put it. But here it is, Henry.

Wherever you are now, dear brother, I hope you enjoy this. The boy who was once lost and alone at the edge of the world is now in the center, in a proper book, telling his own story.

1.

Before the Fall

Once again, a book open in front of him, a sea of letters floating before his eyes, the sweat forming on his brow, the pain in his stomach like he's being punched from the inside. And the whole class around him, holding their breath, waiting for him to read out loud, waiting to burst out laughing. But he's not going to read. Not now or ever. He's going to wait, like the last time and the time before that, like in the last school and the school before that. He's going to stay silent.

"Henry, we're waiting," the teacher says impatiently, a hint of threat in his voice.

He's not sure how this teacher will react to his silence. Shout? Wait? Sometimes they sent him out of the classroom. That's what he's hoping for now; that's all he wants. To leave, so he can be alone. No more people, no more words.

Was this school number six or seven? He wasn't sure. Soon enough Mom would lose her job, or the apartment, and they would move again.

Maybe it was all because of the way he looked. His tiny eyes and big nose, his small mouth with crooked teeth, his big head with a tuft of coarse red hair. And then there was his clubfoot, crumbling under his weight, as if he was falling over with every step. He had never seen anyone as ugly as himself. Nor had anybody else, it seemed.

The kids never talked to him; they shouted. But he could never reply. And then their words turned cruel. In every school a fresh crowd of pretty boys appeared, with their sweet mouths full of wicked words. Schools taught him nothing but wicked words, to keep his mouth shut, and eventually to fight back.

In the beginning, though, he hadn't fought back. He took the punches and the kicks and the wicked words. He'd kept his mouth shut and his fists clenched. And he learned very quickly to hate himself, even more than everyone else seemed to hate him.

"Where did you get that head of yours? What small eyes you've got! Is your mother a pig? Hey, Dog-face! Pig-face! Rat-face! What's with your leg, Limpy?"

No, he couldn't fight back with words. Talking had never been easy, because he stuttered, fighting the same letter for an eternity. His tongue tripped up sounds as they made their way out.

Back in the classroom he would wait in silence until the teacher got mad or threw him out. No matter how hard they tried, no teacher had managed to get him to utter a single word from a book, not that he could remember anyway.

Besides, he couldn't read. The letters swam before his eyes, changing their places in the lines, so he had to chase them around the page while his heart punched hard against his chest and sweat poured down his face. He knew them, of course, and the sounds they were supposed to make, but from *his* mouth they sounded wrong. His writing was clumsy and full of mistakes too, but it didn't matter to him.

And there would always be a new school anyway. What was the point? A fresh start, his mother called it, but it was the same for him everywhere. There was never a fresh start for him, because he couldn't change.

And here he was again in a new school. This time it wasn't because Mom had lost her job or the apartment, but because he'd finally snapped. And it had made him feel better than he'd ever felt in his whole life.

He'd been sitting alone as usual when it happened, in the corner of the playground, by the concrete wall, which was hidden from the school. The kids called it the "swear-wall" because it was covered in rude graffiti. Large, bright letters spelled out the worst words the kids could think of. Sitting here he almost felt invisible, and therefore secure, watching the kids run around the playground.

It had been a Friday, but this Friday was different from the others, for it was his birthday. Of course nobody knew that except him. It didn't make him feel happy, but it made him somehow softer on the inside. He remembered some good times with his mother. When she'd looked much younger, almost beautiful, and how she had smiled when she'd handed him a present. How happy she'd been seeing him so excited. Now she didn't smile anymore. And he knew it was his fault.

The bell rang, but he was slow to get up.

Suddenly the playground was empty, except for a group of

older boys inching toward him, laughing mockingly, looking forward to their little game with him, right behind that concrete wall, where the teachers in the staff room wouldn't be able to see them.

He tried to quicken his pace, but his clubfoot slowed him down. They pushed him around, mocking him. Oh, how they longed for him to cry and beg for mercy. But he swallowed the lump of fright in his throat; his eyes were dry and his mouth was shut. Even when they pulled the tuft of red hair on his monstrous head, nothing happened. He just clenched his fists and took the kicks.

But then one of them said something about his mom. Later he couldn't even remember what the boy had said, he just remembered this one thought, this powerful emotion rushing through him: attack!

He rose up screaming like an animal and pounded his clenched fists into the face closest to him. He felt jawbone smashing under his thick knuckles. The boy fell to the ground, and Henry kicked him hard in the stomach, again and again with his heavy, specially made clubfoot shoe, all the time screaming at the top of his voice; a horrifying sound, like a crazy cartoon monster or a wild beast howling. The others backed away, suddenly terrified, then fled while Henry stood over his victim like a monster from hell set on devouring its prey. He felt immensely large and strong; his anger had the power of a bulldozer, his fists could go through walls.

But the boy who he'd attacked had proper parents who demanded a meeting with the principal. Even with his jaw wired the pretty boy managed to describe in detail how Henry had attacked him for no reason at all, sweet tears streaming from his bright, innocent eyes. The other boys confirmed his story. Henry had nothing to say. He just felt extremely happy with his newfound strength. He didn't have the rich vocabulary, the sober mind of a kid from a proper home with proper parents, to describe the event from his point of view. And he didn't care. His fists had spoken. He smiled a little without meaning to, a feeling of contentment within, but it looked like a malicious grin to the principal and the parents. Henry was the guilty one. And it felt immensely good.

After that they'd moved to another part of town. And now he was here, at another school, and he wasn't going to give anyone the pleasure of mocking him because of his stuttering speech. No, he was going to endure in silence until the teacher threw him out.

2.

The Evil Boy

Then a day came when Henry really exploded, and did the most horrible thing.

He was brought to an institution, a short-term center for young criminals, junkies and the like, for them to decide where to send him next. His room was locked at night and he spent his days in the psychologist's office.

Sitting for two hours every day with the psychologist was actually rather pleasant. Henry was relieved that the psychologist called him only by his first name, instead of using the whole row of names he was christened by, the names his mom had chosen for him to suffer under: Henry William Richard Charles.

She'd said these were the names of his fathers, but even he knew that a person could only have one father. Maybe she wasn't sure herself who his father was. There had been so many men: staying for a while, but then leaving suddenly. None of them kind, all of them ugly. Sometimes he hated her for her stupidity and ignorance, her vulnerability, her lack of strength, how fragile she was, how lonely and so utterly lost, sobbing quietly in her troubled dreams in the night, like a child that's been unjustly punished.

But when she was awake, she never shed a tear. When he was still small enough for her to scold him for something he'd done, she said that crying wouldn't change a thing.

"Life is as it is and crying won't make it better," she said. "Never let me see you cry again. It's useless."

That's about the only thing he learned from her: not to cry.

But he didn't tell the psychologist about that. The guy tried to be nice and friendly, but he was impatient: he wanted answers. When he asked Henry to explain why he did this or why he hadn't done that, his voice was calm enough, but his eyes pressed him for an answer.

"So, tell me, Henry; why did you attack your mother? Take your time. There's no hurry."

It was such a simple question, but there was no simple answer.

She had been pleading with him to behave in school, never again to fight back. "I'm too tired to move again," she'd said. "Soon I'll be too old to get a decent job anywhere; you don't want your mother to be a cleaner in her old age, now, do you?"

He didn't. So he promised to behave, no matter what, promised to take the beatings and the insults so they would never have to move again.

At first he thought it would be easy; after all, that's what he'd done most of his life. But now he had changed; he'd found his strength and experienced the joy of victory.

7

When he lay still in the darkness of his room at night, he could hear their dark, threatening voices echo in his head, accompanied by the distant laughter and happy, playful sounds of the schoolyard in the background. He felt a pain in his stomach and an uncontrollable tingling in his legs, like he needed to run, very fast, very far.

But he couldn't run because of his clubfoot, and he couldn't fight back because of his promise. Week by week, a dark power grew steadily inside him. And, slowly but surely, it began to turn against his mom.

After all, she had denied him the pleasure of fighting back, now of all times, when he knew that he could crush his enemies. *Now* she made him promise to do nothing.

Eventually, the evening came when she had to pay the price for bringing him into this world. Later he couldn't recall what triggered it—her whining voice, her frail body hunched over the kitchen sink, the lousy food on the table in front of him. Maybe all of this and then some other things as well, darker things, distant memories from childhood, bottled up inside him, ready to explode.

He remembered throwing the table over and smashing a wooden chair against the kitchen wall. He remembered the terror in her eyes. She tried to grab his hands to hold him still, push him into a chair; she shouted for him to stop it. But he caught her by the arm, twitching it hard so it snapped, fragile as a bird's bone. She fell on the floor, screaming in pain, and then he was scared.

He limped all through the night, around the docks, hitting

and kicking everything in his path. Cursing, hissing, growling, banging his fists furiously on the rough concrete walls until his knuckles bled. He was terrified of the anger boiling inside of him. It had taken control of him, possessed him like the devil.

During the night he hid in an old, wrecked car in the junkyard, right next to the docks. When morning came he didn't dare go home. He dragged himself to school, perhaps hoping that when he came home in the afternoon, everything would be back to normal, somehow; that it had just been a bad dream.

When he arrived in the schoolyard everyone was already inside. The bell had rung for the last time, so he sat down in the playground. The windows were full of curious faces looking at him, their mouths moving fast, their eyes wide with terror. Maybe everyone already knew what he had done. But he really didn't care what happened next.

The police arrived to pick him up and he went with them willingly. He went to the station, where they took his photograph and fingerprints. Then he was brought to this place, this institution for young criminals, and he spent his days sitting with the nice psychologist who did most of the talking to begin with. But then the psychologist expected Henry to give some answers, and there were no easy answers to his questions.

The guy tapped his fingers on his writing pad. Henry sighed and finally came up with an answer he imagined the psychologist would like.

"I'm evil."

The man just nodded. A few days later he'd finished his report. He didn't declare Henry retarded, not in the strict clinical sense of the word. He wrote that the boy obviously had difficulties expressing himself, but seemed to understand much more than he was able to express.

Henry has been a victim of bullying for a long time, and this has seriously affected his social skills. He does not mix well with other children and has limited linguistic abilities. Bullying and neglect seem to have colluded to give Henry low self-esteem and the impression that he is evil. This conflict of comprehension, without the skills for expression, perhaps explains his violent outbursts of uncontrollable rage.

One day the warden told Henry he had a visitor. He was hoping it was Mom, but when the warden led him into the visiting room he saw a man in a gray suit, sitting at the table.

He stared at Henry for a long time, with a kind smile. "Henry, your mother can't care for you anymore." He waited again, maybe hoping for a reaction. "Do you understand what that means?"

Henry nodded.

"The state will take care of all your needs now."

Then he told Henry he was going to be sent to a lovely home in the beautiful countryside, where so many boys had become better men through the years.

"It's called the Home of Lesser Brethren." He smiled. "It's a proper farm, run by a good Christian couple," he said, reading from a paper in his hands. "And they have lovely animals there," he added. "Sheep, I believe—and cows even! I'm sure you'll feel much better there," he said warmly, his eyes glowing with sincerity.

He talked about the freedom of the countryside, the beautiful scenery, the peace and the quiet. He made it sound as if he regretted terribly that he couldn't go there himself, as if Henry should be counting his lucky stars that he'd gotten this opportunity, as if he was being rewarded. But Henry knew he was being sent away because he was trouble, because he was evil; he was being sent to the edge of the world so nobody would have to worry about him anymore.

3.

The Home of Lesser Brethren

Henry had been staring through the window for two hours, but the landscape hadn't changed since the bus had left the city behind. It had rained constantly; the sky was dark and gray. Black, brown, and gray slabs of lava stretched out as far as the eye could see. Occasionally there were heaps of huge boulders, like ruins of an ancient city. But no human hand had made this landscape; the whole peninsula had been formed by volcanic eruptions in ages past, the government official by his side told him, eager to explain the geological wonder that surrounded them.

"Imagine," he said with wide eyes, "layer upon layer of red-hot lava gushing up from the bowels of the earth, flowing over everything in its path, until it cooled down, enough to slow to a stop. Then, years later, tiny shrubs of vegetation took root. The moss is a stubborn thing." He gave Henry a knowing smile. "It doesn't give up easily. Though storms and rain threaten to wash it away, green or yellow or gray, the moss is the only organism that has truly conquered the lava," he concluded with a proud look on his face, like he was responsible for this remarkably talented plant.

Henry breathed on the window, hoping the man had finished. He felt terrible, like he was about to explode. He missed his mom. He'd never been away from her before, and he'd barely caught a glimpse of her in the rain through the bus window as it drove off from the station. She had been too late. *Too late, Mom. How could you?*

Waves of anxiety washed over him again and again, and he trembled like he was freezing. His eyes felt warm, but he forced back the tears with all his might and bit his lip so hard it bled, clenching his fists in his lap. Why had she let them send him away? He was trying hard to focus on something, anything, but the blabbering official made it impossible. Finally he fixed his eyes on the bus driver, trying to imagine himself behind the steering wheel. It looked easy enough; perhaps that would be the perfect job for him some day.

The official continued, "Eventually, birds bring seeds with their droppings; thick short grass finds shelter between the boulders; tiny flowers decorate the vast desert with their colorful little faces. And then the insects arrive. Age after age, a thin layer of soil will form and the occasional birch tree will have the courage to grow into a tangled shrub. Heather, angelica, and fern bring the finishing touches to this delicate painting, which life itself has been working on for ages," he said with a sigh and a smile.

In his mind, Henry grabbed the man's throat with both hands and squeezed hard, hard, hard, screaming at him to shut up, shut up, shut up; then ripped his head off and threw the corpse far into his beloved lava field. Henry forced himself to close his eyes, hoping the man would think he was sleeping. But he didn't.

"Then, suddenly, a new eruption takes place," he said with fresh excitement. Henry let his chin drop slowly down to his chest, feigning sleep. "Burning lava covers everything once again, poisonous sulfur fills the air, the lava flows over the hills like a waterfall, incinerating everything in its path."

The man paused and then finally shut up.

Henry didn't find the lava interesting at all; it was just ground, earth, surface. It reminded him of burned porridge, chunky, heavy, and clotted. Here and there, large rocks thrust their threatening knuckles up through the thick gray moss. In other places huge cracks cut through the surface, revealing deep crevasses, black bottomless pits, like open mouths of sleeping giants. If anyone should fall in, they'd never get back out. Maybe that was exactly what everybody hoped would happen to him.

Finally the bus turned off the main road and eased down a crooked gravel road toward a farm.

The buildings stood on a grassy knoll surrounded by a vast lava field, like an island of green in the middle of a stormy ocean, the black waves forever frozen in time. The farmhouse was a white, two-story concrete building with a low red roof. Around the house was a garden wall with an iron gate. Inside the wall were several trees, trying to grow tall. Across the yard there were stables: a large barn with four smaller structures facing the farmyard. West of the barn stood a garage and a smithy.

The rain had finally eased, but the air was cold. In the middle of the yard stood a tall cairn, built of lava rocks, with a white iron cross on top. Henry noticed a small gray bird perched on it briefly, waving its long black tail, chirping. Bird and boy pondered each other for a moment.

A tall man in a suit stepped out of the farmhouse.

His shoes were shining as he walked across the yard. He exchanged a few words with the government official and signed some papers. Then he turned and greeted Henry with a firm handshake.

"And you are Henry." He had a groomed beard and gold-rimmed glasses. "Welcome to your new home," he said firmly. "I'm Reverend Oswald."

It was chilly standing outside, and Henry felt awkward. He wasn't used to shaking hands with men in suits, not used to handshakes in general. It felt stupid. And the man's cologne tickled his nostrils. He didn't look like a farmer at all, in his smart suit and shiny shoes with his spicy aftershave. But then Henry had never been out of the city and had no idea what farmers looked like. And he didn't care, didn't care at all. He just wanted to jump back on the bus, start the engine, and drive off. The bus driver leaned against the tall cairn with a grin, gnawing the tip of his pipe, the gray smoke whirling around his head. Why was he grinning? Why was everybody so cheerful?

"You'll be fine," the official said as he climbed back on the bus.

"Yeah, you've come to the right place," the driver said

before he closed the doors and started the engine. But his eyes were mean; the smell of his tobacco lingered in the air, mixing with the reverend's spicy cologne and the diesel fumes from the bus as it drove off along the dusty road. Suddenly Henry felt sick. He needed to throw up. But he didn't. He clenched his jaw, forcing himself to hold back. His eyes searched for the small gray bird with the long black tail. But it was gone.

Reverend Oswald patted him on the shoulder and said he would introduce him to his wife, Emily. She would help him settle in.

Then he showed Henry into the kitchen and disappeared.

Henry didn't know what to expect next. A kitchen full of nasty troublemakers like himself, perhaps, ready to attack, to tear him apart with their wicked words, their clenched fists and angry shouts? Perhaps more psychologists asking more questions, questions, questions.

But it was nothing like that.

The sun had been bright outside, so for a few seconds the kitchen seemed utterly dark. But there was this wonderful smell he'd never smelled before, and the sound of batter being poured gently into a frying pan, where it crackled briefly in melted butter, giving off an amazing scent. And Henry realized he didn't feel sick anymore; he just felt hunger, healthy hunger.

The woman standing by the stove glanced over her shoulder and smiled. Her voice was soft, almost a whisper.

"Hi, there. Come in. I'm almost finished with this one. You must be famished. Have a seat beside the stove, and I'll get you a mug of coffee. There's nothing like warm rye pancakes with butter, and fresh coffee after a long journey."

She took his hand in both of hers and bid him welcome with a warm smile on her rosy cheeks. She was slightly plump, with long auburn hair tied in a knot, and her breasts were heavy and round under her cotton blouse. Henry noticed that her big blue eyes didn't flinch nor did her sweet smile freeze with terror when she looked at him, as so often happened when people saw him for the first time.

Emily offered to take his jacket, with a small movement of her hands, as if he was an honored guest. She showed him where the bathroom was, if he wanted to freshen up after the bus drive. "But if I were you, I'd dive into the rye pancakes while they're warm," she said with a gleam in her eye. She dipped a ladle into the batter again and gently poured another portion into the frying pan.

Henry sat in the chair by the warm stove, folded his fingers around the coffee mug, and breathed in the wondrous scent. Emily put a large chunk of butter on a pancake, spread it with a knife, and immediately the butter melted down. She cut the pancake in two and handed him the plate. "There," she said softly. "I hope you like it."

The warm pancake, soaked with melted butter, tasted even better than it smelled; its softness on the tongue, the mild taste of cinnamon or herbs or something, sent a gentle shiver through him, a rush of pleasure he'd never felt. Before he knew it, he had finished the pancake, and without saying a word she buttered another one and put it on his plate.

Emily continued her work in silence, occasionally buttering another pancake for him or offering him more coffee with only a questioning smile. He had expected questions, interrogation even, the usual treatment he'd had from new teachers in the past: What's your favorite subject? Could you read this for me? Can you write your name? Are you always so quiet? Speak up, or you'll get what's coming to you!

But maybe she wasn't a teacher. He almost wanted to ask her. But he didn't. This silence was far too precious to spoil it with a stupid question.

His anxiety had melted away, just like the butter on the warm rye pancakes. He felt at peace, sitting here on the chair by the stove, coffee mug in his hand, the sweet taste in his mouth. The quiet, gentle woman went about her business in the kitchen as if he wasn't even there, while making him feel more welcome than he'd felt anywhere.

Henry realized he had never been in a room with another person without feeling any pressure at all. He just felt at ease, such as he had only felt occasionally, especially when he was awake in the middle of the night, safe in the darkness of his room, safe under his warm duvet, when the morning was still too far away for his anxiety to stir.

It was a relief but so very strange at the same time; he had only just arrived, furious on the inside, frozen on the outside, like so many times before, and then suddenly this chair, the pancakes, the warm stove, the gentle woman. And he was at ease like never before, like he belonged here. Whatever happened next, he wouldn't freak out. He was certain.

But there were still the other boys to consider. And the reverend. Remembering the cold eyes behind the gold-rimmed glasses made Henry feel frightened all over again. Frightened, lost, and alone.

From outside, the sound of chatter and running feet approached, and the kitchen door was flung open, so it hit the wall with a loud bang. Emily turned abruptly, staring at the two boys standing there; one sniffing because his nose was running, the other sniffing the scent of the pancakes. They were about nine years old, eleven at the most. Henry breathed in slowly, filling his lungs, preparing for the worst. He tried to sit up straight so he'd seem bigger; perhaps they were young enough to be scared of him. Suddenly they noticed him, sitting there by the stove, and their faces froze. Then he knew. They wouldn't give him any trouble. Not yet.

"You do not enter a house in this manner," Emily said, without raising her voice one bit. They lowered their heads, the one with the running nose whispering, "Sorry, Miss Emily, but we just wanted to ask if . . ."

"First you knock. Then you wait for a reply, and then you open the door, but gently, Timothy. Please."

"Yes, Miss Emily."

Timothy reached for the doorknob and left, closing the door without a sound. Then they heard a timid knock.

"Come in," Emily said, winking at Henry and smiling.

Timothy opened the door.

"Miss Emily, can Paul and me—"

"Paul and I," Emily corrected.

"Can Paul and I play the organ?"

"Of course you can," she said. "But only one at a time. And if anybody else wants to play, they have to ask for my permission first."

"Yes, Miss Emily. Thank you," they said in perfect unison, and closed the door ever so gently.

Emily smiled. "All the other boys are around Paul and Timothy's age. You'll have a better chance to meet them all later; there's no hurry. But if you feel up to it, I'd like to show you to your room now."

Henry breathed out slowly. He wanted to smile as well, but he was afraid she might misunderstand it and take it for a malicious grin like everybody else had always done. So he didn't smile. Not on the outside, anyway.

4.

The King of Dung

"I'll be in the kitchen, if there's anything you need," she said. "Just take your time to settle in. Look around the place if you like. I'll check on you before dinnertime."

Her smile lingered in the air long after she had left the room. Henry sat on his bed, breathing in the smell of clean sheets, the fresh scent of the tiny purple flowers standing in a jar on the chest of drawers by the small window. There was a small table and a chair, a colorful rug on the wooden floor, and a couple of pictures on the wall: photographs of a sunny country somewhere, a vineyard perhaps. And there was a tiny bathroom with a shower.

The room had been built inside the cowshed, some years ago, when they'd had a farmhand, Emily had told Henry. There was plenty of space for the cows, so a portion of the barn had been made into simple living quarters for the farmhand. The man had married a widow on a farm in the district, so now he was the farmer there, but he still helped them out from time to time, mowing the fields, moving the hay into the barn.

"Now that you're here," Emily had said, "your work will

be to feed the cows and clean the stalls and the dung canal. And in a couple of months they will be let out, and you'll herd them to pasture after morning milking and get them back for the evening milking."

At that point a sudden spasm of anxiety had whirled around in his stomach. She must have noticed, for she told him not to worry about anything; she would teach him how to milk.

Then she'd shown him the sheep shed. The sheep turned to the open door, wide eyed, bleating loudly, their purple tongues trembling in their open mouths. The stink of their dung was bitter and nasty.

"The sheep, of course, will have to be fed too," Emily said. "But pretty soon we'll herd them up on the heath where they'll be grazing all summer, so we don't have to worry about them till autumn."

The door and the window frame in his room were painted white, the walls dark green; a pleasant color that made him somehow feel secure. The soft spicy scent of the hay in the barn tickled his nostrils a little. From the other side of the wall he heard the cows sigh and murmur to themselves, and an occasional bleat from the sheep shed, next door. A low rumbling could be heard in the distance, almost like thunder, but regular like a heartbeat.

From the window, the vast lava field stretched as far as the eye could see. In the distance Henry caught a glimpse of columns of white foam shooting high into the air: the ocean waves exploding on the cliffs. The rumbling he'd heard was the heartbeat of the ocean. He felt tired and a little dizzy. His eyelids were heavy and the soothing rumble was like a lullaby. He rocked his body gently back and forth. Then he lay on the bed, fully clothed, and didn't even bother to take his shoes off. He fell asleep, instantly, and slept like a babe in a crib, while the sunbeams moved ever so slowly across the colorful rug on the wooden floor.

He dreamed he was flying, high in the air; the buildings on the farm like toy houses in the middle of the vast lava field, far below him. He was a bird, a small gray bird with a long black tail. The lava field suddenly became liquid, moving like waves on the ocean; surf made of huge boulders falling around the tiny buildings. It was like the end of the world. He noticed Emily climbing the tall cairn in the middle of the yard, clinging to the white cross on top, crying, "Help me, Henry! Please, help me!" He dived down and realized he wasn't a small bird after all, but a big bird, big enough for her to climb on his back. "Where to?" he chirped. "Home," she said. "Let's go home."

She woke him up before dinner and he limped behind her toward the house, dizzy, confused, and sleepy. Twenty little boys stood silently by their chairs around a long table in the dining room. At the head of the table stood Reverend Oswald. Steam rose from a large plate of boiled fish, a bowl full of potatoes, and another bowl full of boiled vegetables. Emily placed a comforting hand on Henry's shoulder.

"This is Henry," she said, and smiled at the boys. "He's our new farmhand and you will show him respect and courtesy."

"Welcome, Henry," said Reverend Oswald, and the boys echoed his greeting in unison: "Welcome, Henry!"

Like a disciplined group of little soldiers, the boys took their seats, clasped their hands in prayer, and rested their foreheads on their knuckles. Emily pulled out a chair for Henry. Then she sat down and indicated that he should bow his head as well and clasp his hands. The reverend drew breath and then words began to flow out of his mouth; his passionate tone of voice rising, increasing in volume and power until the words were bouncing off the dining-room walls, hitting Henry's eardrums like fists, pounding his ears.

"God Almighty! Heavenly Father! Your Grace Knows No Limits! Your Mercy Is Boundless! Your Love Is The Breath We Breathe! The Beating Of Our Hearts! The Very Soul Of Our Being! You Are Our Father! And We Are Your Children! Humbly We Thank You, O Lord, For Everything You Have Given And For What We Are About To Receive! Amen!"

"Amen!" the boys cried.

Then utter silence, until the reverend took a piece of fish, put it on his plate, and everyone began to eat.

No one said anything; the only sounds were when a fork or a knife touched a plate, an occasional cough or a sneeze, or when someone cleared his throat as quietly as possible. And because of this silence the last words spoken by Reverend Oswald were somehow still flying around the dining room, growing louder and louder in Henry's head with every minute. Henry finished eating before everybody else and fixed his eyes on Emily, screaming his own prayer, asking that he might leave the table. But she didn't look up, and he dared not move.

He glanced around the table. The official had told him on

the bus that most of the boys here came from troubled families, their moms or dads either in prison or in mental institutions. Some of the boys had been caught stealing, robbing shops, breaking and entering. A few had no parents at all and were waiting to be taken in by foster parents. Some had wide eyes full of sadness, like it would take nothing to make them start crying. Others had cold eyes and hard faces, as if nothing could surprise them anymore. They were like grown men; perhaps they had experienced too much, too soon. Henry imagined that the sad ones still believed that everything would be all right one day, even though every day of their short lives had been nothing but disappointing. They still had hope. The hard ones had exchanged childish dreams for something more durable: hate.

Henry could sense their anger. He'd been hopeful once, and later full of hate. And now? Now he was a little confused, because of Emily and her kindness. He wasn't ready to hope for anything just yet though. No, not at all. He would cling to his hate a little longer, just to be on the safe side. Besides, he didn't know what to think about the reverend. He was cold all right, harsh, strict, with his mouth full of words, complicated words, terrifying words.

Finally dinner was over and Henry limped behind Emily to the cowshed. The routine was simple: "First you fetch them fresh hay. Then you scrape the stalls clean and shovel out the dung canal. You empty the wheelbarrow into the heap behind the barn," Emily explained. "I'll do the milking tonight, but tomorrow morning I'll teach you how to do it."

Henry liked the cows at once.

They were big and clumsy like he was, lazy and annoyed: Old Red, Little Gray, Spotty with her large horns, Brandy and Belle; there were Jenny, Maggy, and Nelly. They rose in their stalls and mooed in deep, gentle voices, craving fresh fodder, like little children begging for candy. There was something so soothing about the way they snorted out clouds of warm breath, the sound of their slow munching, their deep grunts of pleasure, and their large, dome-shaped eyes gleaming with carefree happiness.

Then there was the bull. It had no name.

Emily warned Henry to be careful because the bull was always angry and not at all fond of people; it could as easily crush a man as a person can squash a fly under their thumb, she said. She seemed terrified of the bull, even though she had been raised on a farm herself. All around the bull's stall was a high wooden fence that reached Henry's chin. When he peeked over it he could just see the black hide. The bull kicked the fence and bellowed angrily. Henry jumped back in fright, his clubfoot crumbling under him so he almost fell to the floor.

"You'd better leave it alone," Emily said.

She sat on a small stool beside one of the cows, washed its udders with hot water, and applied grease to the teats before she began milking. A white stream of pure milk hit the inside of the bucket, and the cow sighed with pleasure.

Henry grabbed the shovel and turned to the dung canal. The cow dung had a soft, sweet smell. As soon as he began, one of the cows raised her tail in the air and shit, like she'd been given a signal. Henry shoveled it up and moved his wheelbarrow along. He was the King of Dung, collecting the dues from his subjects, filling the wheelbarrow. He pushed the heavy load around the barn, where he emptied it onto the heap in one quick movement.

He breathed in the salty wind coming off the ocean. He felt great. He was a farmhand, a workingman. He was somebody. Who would have thought? The King of Dung couldn't help but smile a little before turning back inside the cowshed to his subjects.

5.

Words of Terror, Words of Magic

Breakfast, lunch, and dinner were all in the dining room of the farmhouse. Reverend Oswald would say a prayer, and then everyone would eat in silence. Every day the boys had classes with Emily in the garage, which was both a makeshift classroom and a chapel. Henry was relieved when Emily told him he didn't have to attend her lessons; he was welcome, of course, but it was not a duty.

But there was no way out of Reverend Oswald's religious lessons. And Henry hated them. When Oswald asked questions, the little ones would compete to answer as fast as they could. Henry wondered if the reverend thought he was retarded, because he never asked him anything, which was the only relief. Oswald's preaching frightened Henry. He spoke so fast that Henry usually didn't have the faintest idea what he was talking about. All that screaming and shouting; if heaven was anything like this, Henry definitely didn't want to go there. He'd never seen a grown man shout with such burning conviction before, like a madman watching a soccer game.

Henry didn't like being among the little boys. None of them were ever going to become his friend, and he didn't care about that; he'd never had any friends anyway. He just wanted to be on his own.

Sunday services were no better.

When everybody had taken their seat, Emily started to play the pedal organ and the boys began to sing. Reverend Oswald sat still with a bowed head and clasped hands, in silent prayer. When the song was over he stood up and started to preach.

He talked a lot about God. But he talked even more about the devil. He said he loved God but hated the devil, for the devil was always trying to get inside people and take control of them. The devil had to be driven out, so people could go to heaven after they died, instead of going to hell. He talked like that, on and on, faster and louder, until finally he was almost screaming and at last he shouted, "Hallelujah!"

And the little ones echoed his shout with fervor.

"No one is without sin," he said. "And those who don't repent will never enter heaven. That's why you are here: to learn how to repent. I know," he continued, "that many have already given up on you, and for good reason too." He looked over the small crowd with his cold blue eyes. "But God will never give up on you and neither will I. The devil may have dug his claws into you, but I will set you free in the name of Jesus! Praise the Lord! Hallelujah!" he shouted, and the boys cried, "Hallelujah!"

Reverend Oswald said that when the devil started to take control of a boy, he had to be punished. What the devil hated most was rebuilding the cairn in the yard, the Cairn of Christ. The punishment started in the evening by taking the top stone from the cairn, and then, one by one, making a cairn just the same next to the old one, stone by stone, before sunrise next morning.

But if the devil had really taken control of a boy, there was one punishment that was much worse. The boy would be locked in the Boiler Room, with no food, to pray, for as long as it took. The devil hated to be starved and hated praying on his knees for days on end.

"Some of you here have rebuilt the Cairn of Christ, and a few of you have been put in the Boiler Room," the reverend said, looking over the crowd. "To begin with, you thought that you were being punished, and you cried and begged on your knees and you promised to be good. But when you had finished rebuilding the Cairn of Christ, when you had spent a few days and nights in the Boiler Room, you finally realized that you weren't the ones being punished, but the devil! And because you humbled yourselves before the Lord, the devil gave up! You were saved and brought back to life in union with Jesus Christ! Hallelujah!"

"Hallelujah!" the boys replied.

After that, Oswald said a long prayer, then Emily pressed the pedals on the organ with her feet and raised her voice in song. The little ones sang with her.

If you're happy and you know it clap your hands.
If you're happy and you know it clap your hands.
If you're happy and you know it and you really want to show it,
if you're happy and you know it clap your hands.

After every service Oswald's words echoed in Henry's head for a long time. They fluttered about in his mind with great speed like screeching birds, inches from colliding into one another; shouting words, whispering words, never-ending sentences that he didn't understand, and then short sharp words, like slaps in the face. Sometimes he didn't fall asleep until early morning from the racket in his head.

His anxiety flexed its muscles; it was like a troll, punching him on the inside with fists, gnawing at his heart. He woke up screaming from nightmares that were full of angry words. He was covered in sweat, trembling with fear.

Lying awake, breathing in the spicy scent of hay and cow dung, Henry thought about stealing away in the night. Maybe he would fall into a deep pit in the lava and never get back out. Perhaps he would die there. Then nobody would have to worry about him anymore. But then he thought of Emily; she would worry. She wouldn't want him to run away. She was a good person. Besides, where on earth would he go? There was no place for him anywhere in the world but here.

Still trembling from his bad dreams, he limped out of his room and into the cowshed. The cows looked at him with their large eyes full of surprise, as if they were thinking, *Isn't it too early for milking?* Some of them rose in their stalls, sniffing toward him, as if murmuring gently, *Go back to sleep, boy.*

Henry stood on the edge of the dung canal and peed.

Suddenly there was a great noise behind him, from the bull's stall; heavy breathing and loud kicking as the monstrous animal rose to its feet.

Henry fell back as a gigantic black head appeared above the fence with an angry frown over its burning eyes. The bull rested its jawbones on the fence and stared at him with its big flappy ears outstretched, spread its nostrils, and knitted its brow. Henry was paralyzed for a moment, overwhelmed by that powerful force of nature measuring him with its angry eyes.

They stared at each other like that for a long time until the black bull suddenly shot its long wet tongue out of its mouth and dug it deep into each of its huge nostrils.

At first Henry was startled, for it happened so suddenly and it seemed completely out of character: the huge, threatening monster picking its nose with its tongue! Henry couldn't help but laugh, a deep, coarse, limping laughter. There was something that tickled him deep inside as he looked at this huge beast with such a dumb expression on its face.

When the bull saw him laugh, it stretched its head forward and curled its upper lip, causing deep wrinkles to form in the skin above its nostrils and exposing its pink, toothless upper gums. Henry mimicked it and curled his upper lip, breathed hard out of his nose like the bull did, and stretched his neck forward. They stood like this for a while, laughing silently into each other's faces.

Henry slipped his hand between the bars and scratched the bull's chin. A deep purr resounded from within the animal, and it closed its eyes gently. He isn't bad, Henry thought. He's not evil; he's just a little angry being fenced in like this. He's not bad, not bad at all. Just lonely. He just needs a friend.

Henry stepped up onto the fence and embraced the bull's head, while the bull tried to eat Henry's sweater with his coarse tongue.

"Good bull," Henry whispered. "Good bull."

He scratched the bull behind the ears, dug his thick fingers into the curls on his forehead. And the bull purred like a kitten.

Henry wanted to give him a name. He remembered that Reverend Oswald had talked about a great flood the other day, about Noah's ark and all the animals. Noah! That was a good name.

Noah purred and pressed himself against the creaking fence, which closed him in on all sides. Carefully, Henry climbed into his stall, squeezing himself into a corner, and stood eye to eye with the bull. Noah sniffed his clothes and pressed his head against Henry's chest. Henry gasped for breath and saw red, but he wasn't going to give up. He embraced the large head and squeezed tightly like he was trying to wring Noah's neck. But Henry knew full well that he wasn't strong enough to do that. And Noah knew it as well; he rolled his eyes and turned his head to the side, with a hint of a grin around his mouth. It was just a little game between two friends, two kindred spirits who had found each other in the loneliness of the world.

When Henry heard footsteps on the gravel outside at dawn, he climbed back over the fence and waited. It was the last day Emily would be helping him milk. She arrived with a smile and a bucket full of hot water. He would be doing all the milking this morning; she said she would only be observing, making sure he was comfortable being left on his own in the cowshed from now on.

He washed Old Red's udders, put grease on the teats, and started milking. Emily looked around and noticed he had scraped all the stalls clean.

"They're so happy when their stalls are clean and dry," she said. "And they give more milk when they're happy," she added.

Henry wondered how to tell her that the bull wasn't really that dangerous, that he was just miserable and lonely. But he had difficulty forming the sentence in his mind, a sentence she would understand. Perhaps it would be best not to tell her, not just yet. Maybe she wouldn't understand, being so afraid of the bull and all.

So he said nothing.

Emily asked him how he felt these days, if everything was all right, if he was happy with his room. He nodded and grunted a sort-of yes, deep in his throat.

"I know this place can be lonely at times," she said, staring out of the small window. "Isolated, perhaps, especially in winter. But the summers here are lovely, you'll see."

They were both silent for a while.

Henry poured the first bucket into a container, which floated in a tank full of cold water, and moved the milking stool next to Little Gray.

With Emily around, Henry never felt pressured; it was always relaxing.

"Ages ago, back in pagan times, there were green meadows where the lava fields are today," Emily said in a low voice, as if talking to herself.

"An eruption cleared the entire area overnight. The lava ran down the mountains in the north, flowed over the fields, and surrounded the knoll where the old farmhouse stood."

For a moment Henry feared that she was about to give him the same lecture he'd been forced to listen to on the bus. But as she continued speaking in her soft voice, her words had a very different effect on him than he had expected.

She told him how the burning lava had rushed over the outbuildings and chased the sheep and the people, who fled toward the sea cliffs and threw themselves over the edge.

Then hundreds of years went by.

Long after the lava had cooled down, there were foreign ships anchoring in the bay below the cliffs, the same bay that came to be known as Shipwreck Bay. Farmers from the countryside traded with the sailors and sold them dried fish and meat, which they transported on horses, their heavy hooves gradually chiseling a path that wound across the lava field.

About midway it passed the Gallows, two boulders that rose high up above the lava and leaned against each other.

"They remind me of two friends bidding each other farewell for the last time," Emily said, almost whispering. "They used to hang thieves and murderers there, you know. It should be a terrible place, but to me it isn't."

Then she told him the old stories of poor young women who, century after century, had come here in the night to hide little bundles away in the maze of holes and caves in the lava field.

"That's the only thing that makes me sad about this place," she said. "Knowing that so many little babies were brought out here to die because nobody could take care of them. And the poor unmarried women would have been punished with their lives if the truth had been known. How hard it must have been for them, how terribly hard and unjust."

At this point in the story she fell silent for a while, and Henry thought there was nothing more to tell. He poured the milk from the bucket into the container without thinking, washed Brandy's udders, and continued milking in a steady rhythm. His mind was ablaze with images from her story. It was like watching a painting come alive.

When Emily spoke again her voice was much brighter and happier, as if she had just needed a little moment to gather her thoughts.

"But then a young farmer came from another part of the country and built the house on the knoll. He also built the garden wall and planted the trees in the yard. He built the barn and the cowshed and sheep sheds. He was a hardworking man, and he laughed when the old people in the countryside told him that the place was cursed.

"He had a lovely wife and many children. Every summer he drove a tractor with a wagon to the faraway fields out east to mow them and then moved the hay back to the barn. It was hard work, but they were happy.

"He had a boat," Emily said, "and moved it from the

smithy, all the way along the path through the lava, and put it to sea in Shipwreck Bay. There's no easy way to haul a boat down that steep cliff face, but he managed it, and rowed his boat when the sea was calm and smooth, cast out nets, and filled the boat with fish. Then he pulled the boat back up to the edge so the surf wouldn't crush it when the tide came in. The farmers in the area called him the Miracle Man, because they envied him. None of them had ever tried to row out from these shores, with their steep cliffs and the sea being so rough. But the young farmer was determined to use every means possible to keep his family happy and well fed.

"But then tragedy struck in the most curious manner," Emily said, and again her voice lowered a little.

"One night in the middle of winter, in a freezing blizzard, the farmer woke up from bad dreams. He told his wife to heat up some food, because they would have visitors that night. Then he went out into the blizzard and followed the path until he reached the edge of the cliffs above Shipwreck Bay.

"Out there he saw a huge trawler, a British trawler called *Young Hope,* stuck on a reef and being crushed to pieces by the roaring waves. Some of the crew were already in the water, fighting for their lives in the surf. But the farmer managed to shoot a line out to the ship. Then he climbed down the cliffs and got hold of the men, one by one, and pulled all twelve of them up onto the edge, to safety.

"The blizzard was so thick and the men so weak that they couldn't even walk to the house. So he carried them, one by one, on his back along the path, all the way to the farm, where

37

warm food and steaming hot coffee awaited them. Since then, the path has been called Spine Break Path in memory of this superhuman feat.

"How he knew about the trawler in the surf nobody will ever know, for when the twelfth crew member had been brought into the house the farmer disappeared into the blizzard again and never came back. Of course, the superstitious old people in the district said that the devil had demanded his toll, the thirteenth man.

"The poor widow sold the farm and moved far away with her children," Emily said. "It's almost ten years now since we bought the farm," she added in a low voice. "And since then, no tragedy has ever taken place here, thank God."

She whispered these last words, almost like a prayer.

Henry was dumbstruck. Not because of the superhuman feat of the Miracle Man, although he found that most impressive, but because he had realized that this was the first time anyone had told him a story. A real story of real people who had actually been alive, and their lives had been horrific and hard, happy and sad. Yes, his mom had read him some storybooks when he was little, but she had never told him a real story, told him anything in her own words, like Emily had just done.

Through her gentle voice, rising and descending, he had visualized the farmer and his family in his mind with no effort at all; they had just appeared there, their faces, their happy laughter, their bitter tears. He had almost felt the blizzard on his skin, the weight of the sailors on his own back—and completely forgotten himself. Her words, as if by some strange magic, had brought him into a mysterious new world, out of time and place.

It took him a moment to realize that he was in fact here, in the cowshed, pouring the last bucket of milk into the container.

"You've graduated," Emily said with a sweet smile. "Now you're officially our farmhand, and a proper cowboy as well!"

After she'd left, Henry stood for a long time beside the water tank, listening to the cold water running.

While his mind had been far away on this strange journey, he had milked eight cows, almost without noticing.

6.

A Just Punishment

It was a Sunday, and the reverend was giving the boys hell.

"In the beginning the devil's name was Lucifer," Reverend Oswald said in a thundering voice. "He was one of the arch-angels of the Lord, the angel of light. But he was proud. When the Lord ordered all the angels to bow to his creation, man, Lucifer refused. He said he loved God too much to bow to anyone but him. But the Lord saw into his arrogant heart. He became sad and angry that one of his beloved archangels had allowed himself to become so selfish and proud.

"So the Lord said, 'Be gone!'

"And Lucifer was cast out of heaven and thrown into the deepest darkness, there to endure for thousands of centuries," Reverend Oswald whispered in a threatening voice, his face red and warm, the sweat glistening on his brow.

"He roams the world, full of hate and jealousy toward man, whom he blames for his downfall, and tries to ensnare us so we too will fall from the grace of God. His only goal is to jus-tify his own pride.

"And since he was the first one to fall from the grace of the Lord, he will also be the last finally allowed into heaven.

When all men are saved and all the sins of the world have been forgiven, then, at last, the Lord will send an angel into the abyss. And the angel will say the words that Lucifer has been longing to hear for thousands of centuries: 'Come home.'"

The pedal organ took over; the boys' singing filled the garage. But Henry didn't sing. The words of Reverend Oswald were screeching and shouting and droning inside his head, driving him mad. His heart was pounding against his chest, sweat was running down his back; he wanted to run very fast, very far. He wanted to scream at the top of his voice.

After the service, the boys rushed outside and ran toward the smithy. There was a playground there with a couple of old tractor tires, a seesaw, and a swing. They were building huts, laughing, chatting happily, fooling around, spending their energy.

Henry limped as fast as he could toward the cowshed. It was early afternoon and he had nothing to do, but he had to do something. His head was bursting.

When he reached the cowshed he leaned against the wall, catching his breath.

To the southeast he could see two huge boulders rising into the air, far away. And right there, only a few feet from where he stood, he noticed the path at the edge of the lava field.

The path wound itself around rocks and past deep crevasses, never straight but bending this way and that, endlessly. It wasn't smooth either and it was no broader than a horse would need in order to place one foot in front of the other. Amazing how the hooves of horses had chiseled that groove into the hard rock, age after age.

Henry had a hard time walking down the path. His clubfoot began to hurt and sometimes it got stuck in a crack or between rocks so he had to pull it free with both hands. And all around him mysterious sounds could be heard, a quacking or rattling or wailing; sometimes just a quick chirp, first close by, then farther away.

A deep bellowing could be heard where the furious surf crashed on the steep cliff wall. Halfway to the cliffs he paused by the Gallows to catch his breath. The huge boulders leaned together just as Emily had said: like two friends bidding farewell to each other for the last time.

Finally he reached the sea cliffs, limping along the edge until he came to Shipwreck Bay, where monstrous waves were beating against the remains of the rusty carcass of *Young Hope*.

The wide ocean stretched as far as his eyes could see.

He stood there for a long time, like a troll turned to stone, his clubfoot stuck between the rocks. The wind was cold and fresh, and the air wove between his fingers; a salty spray gently stroked his face. He looked down into the bay at the backs of thousands of white birds that rose in the air on the strong breeze and circled around him, silent and curious. Then they hurled themselves into the void, screeching and calling, then gliding off into the far distance.

The stark blue waves rushed against the cliffs below, with white foam on top, exploding so furiously that the rock trembled underneath him. The deep, deep rumble of the waves, the relentless roar of the ocean; full of sadness or regret somehow, then suddenly full of anger and spite. It foamed like soap down in the bay and moved around the rust-burned corpse of the trawler.

Henry lay down on his stomach, his head over the edge, the cliff underneath him trembling against his heart. He no longer knew where the cliff ended and he took over, where the surf ceased and his heartbeat began. The ocean was so cruel, so overwhelming, so cold and deep, maybe deeper than the height of the sky above him. With a loud roar it banged its fists against the cliffs, snatching the longhaired seaweed with its sharp claws, ripping it from the cliff face, crunching the rocks with its sharp teeth.

The birds swung in the air below him and above him, so white and clean. They were like the words in his head, the words that flew, screeching around, inches from colliding into one another. Following the birds with his eyes, he suddenly realized his head was finally empty of words. There was nothing there but the overwhelming sound of the roaring ocean, almighty and unconquerable.

Why had the words of the reverend hurt him so much? Why had he wanted to jump to his feet and scream: No! You're wrong! You know nothing!

Before he came to this place Henry had only heard Jesus mentioned when somebody was swearing. He'd known next to nothing about God or the devil. But the reverend's sermons had taught him that there is a system in the world, and that God was a kind of king in heaven, who had sent his son, Jesus, to save mankind from the devil. So Henry had imagined that the devil was really evil and everybody should hate him. But now he had been told that the devil was thrown out of heaven because he loved God more than anything. So who was the evil one? The one who threw him out of heaven, or the one who only wanted to have a friend?

The voice of Reverend Oswald had become quiet in his mind, and all the angry words had dispersed among the birds in the cliffs. All that was left was the emptiness of his own soul.

Was it because he felt pitiful, like the archangel turned devil? Longing for a friend, just like that lonely creature in hell? Henry wondered if God would ever send him an angel with some comforting words. But he doubted that would ever happen. Why should the Lord bother with him?

Sitting on the edge of the cliffs, he could see the huge freighters disappearing over the horizon; the long, drawn-out bellow from their foghorns echoed across the vast ocean. It was a sound of regret. It stirred something inside of him and made him sad. Then he thought about his mom.

He remembered the day he'd sat on the bus at the station, the government official sitting beside him, constantly trying to make conversation with him. Henry had just stared out the window, waiting for Mom to bid him farewell. But Mom didn't show up, and the bus slowly began to move.

It had been raining so hard that day. As he peered through the raindrops he suddenly saw her standing in the parking lot, her right arm in a cast. She had wrapped a plastic bag around the cast so it wouldn't get wet. When she saw he had noticed her, she raised her other hand and waved. The man beside him asked if he wasn't going to wave back. But Henry neither wanted to look nor wave. And yet he couldn't take his eyes off her; she was so vulnerable in the cold, with a hat on, dressed in her old coat and wearing her winter boots in the pouring rain.

When the bus finally moved off she started to run beside it, right under the window where he sat. She had waved and sobbed. His mom, who had always taught him that crying made no difference, that crying didn't make things any better, that it was useless to cry. He'd learned that from her. And then she had cried in the broad daylight. And it made him terribly angry.

Once the bus turned out of the parking lot, she stopped running. He could see her in the large side mirror; the plastic bag had blown off and was dancing around her. She grew smaller and smaller until the bus turned again and her image disappeared.

There had been so many hard days, so many bad men; how he had longed to become big and strong so that he could protect her. He had dreams of the two of them, happy and carefree somewhere, with a proper bedroom each, with proper food on the table. But they were always on the move and the houses were gray and small and the happy days never came. And when he had finally become strong enough to protect her, he had hurt her.

45

Somehow, one way or another, everything had been his fault.

The roaring fury of the ocean beneath him echoed in his thoughts: *Your fault! Your fault! Your fault!*

He jumped to his feet and shouted, "No!"

Huge boulders, rocks, and stones of all sizes were strewn around him on the edge of the cliff, thrown up by the powerful waves over the ages. He grabbed one with both hands, raised it high above his head, and threw it over the edge. The birds below swung to the sides as the black rock fell straight into their midst, falling until it disappeared into the frothing waves far below. He found another rock, much too heavy for him to lift, but he could roll it toward the edge if he used all his strength. So he did. His anger made him powerful; his stubby fingers dug themselves into the rock as he pushed.

He roared at the top of his lungs as it plunged over the edge, exploding into a huge wave as it rolled in. He couldn't stop but limped hurriedly toward another rock, even bigger than the last one. With every rock that he pushed over the edge, he felt his strength increase, his anger exploding as the rocks hit the cliffs on the way down, his regret and sadness engulfed by the furious waves.

Somewhere deep down on the ocean floor, these rocks would rest for eternity, preserving inside their thick armor the memory of his emotions, the sound of his voice.

For the first time since he reached the farm, he broke his routine and didn't get back in time for dinner. By the time he limped into the yard it was dark already and he went straight to the cowshed.

Inside, the darkness was thick before his eyes.

Noah stood in his stall, waiting. Maybe he understood exactly how Henry felt. Henry crawled into the stall and took the large bull's head between his hands. But the bull didn't press against him as he usually did when they played this game. He just nudged the crown of his head gently against the boy's chest.

And that was no small sign of compassion from a fully grown bull.

Of course, breaking the rules had consequences.

At breakfast Emily didn't greet him with her usual smile. She just showed him into Reverend Oswald's office.

The reverend was sitting at his desk, leafing through some papers. He didn't look up. Emily pulled out a chair for Henry and closed the door behind her.

There were bookshelves that reached up to the ceiling, bursting with a multitude of folders marked with capital letters. Then there were other shelves full of books. On a lectern in the corner lay an open Bible with a red ribbon between the pages.

The cover on the chair was torn around the armrests. Henry wound up the loose threads, dug his fingers underneath the upholstery, and picked at the stuffing. The room was warm;

the dusty smell of the books tickled his nose. He wanted to sneeze, but he didn't dare. Snot trickled from his nose. He wanted to sniff, but he didn't dare make a sound, so every now and then he shot out his tongue, just like Noah, and licked his upper lip clean.

Finally Reverend Oswald looked up and rested his hands on the desk. His eyes were cold and hard behind the gold-rimmed glasses.

"Where were you yesterday evening?" he asked.

Henry swallowed, and sweat ran down his brow. He opened his mouth a little, not to talk, just to breathe, for his heart was pounding hard.

"Asleep," he finally managed to whisper.

"That is not the truth," the reverend said sternly. "I went to your room myself to look for you, but you weren't there."

Henry felt as if his eyes were popping out of his head. Please, he thought, don't make me rebuild the cairn, don't lock me up in the Boiler Room! He had to think fast to come up with an answer, but thinking up an answer had never been easy for him, least of all under such pressure. His fingers were tearing uncontrollably at the upholstery.

"I-I w-w-was a-at th-the c-c-c-cliffs," he finally said after having fought every word. His voice sounded so funny in his ears; high-pitched, screeching almost, like in a cartoon. The sweat trickled down his back and from under his arms.

The reverend raised an eyebrow in surprise for a second. Then he became angry.

"That's strictly forbidden! It can be dangerous! You are absolutely not allowed to go down to the cliffs. Do you understand?"

Henry shot his tongue upward, licking the snot in a frenzy, digging his fingers into the holes in the armrests.

"There are dangerous pits in the lava, and someone with your walking disabilities shouldn't go there by himself. From the Gallows, Spine Break Path can be dangerous. It is strictly forbidden to go down to the sea cliffs. You might easily be washed out by the waves, or you might slip and fall over the edge! Do you understand?"

Henry nodded eagerly, earnestly, like he wanted nothing more in the world than to obey, like he regretted terribly having been such a fool to follow the path. He wiped the sweat off his face with his arm.

"All right," the reverend said in a milder voice. "We'll speak no more of this. If we follow the rules, we feel good. It's when we break the rules that we start to feel bad. And then we cease to care and we go on breaking the rules until none are left unbroken. You know the Ten Commandments?"

Henry shook his head.

"You'll learn them soon. They are the rules that God himself gave us so we could lead a happy life. It's the same with the rules of our home. If we obey them we can't go wrong. But if we break them . . ." The reverend didn't finish his sentence, as if he was giving Henry a moment to imagine what terrible punishment awaited him if he kept on breaking the rules.

The reverend was silent for a while. Henry sat on the edge of the chair, waiting with his mouth open, trying to calm down, trying to slow his racing heart.

"You're very hardworking, Henry," the reverend said gently. "And you take good care of the cows, Emily tells me. She sent our report to the Welfare Office, and they're quite impressed by your improvement here with us. So I have been wondering if I should investigate whether we could get you into the agricultural college. Would you like me to do that?"

Henry stared at him for a long time, not knowing what to say, how to reply. He wasn't used to being asked his opinion. Least of all about where he would be sent next. Somebody else had always decided that. But now he somehow felt that the reverend was letting him off the hook, releasing him without punishment, setting him free. So he nodded eagerly and breathed out a reply.

"Yeah."

"Of course, you'd have to join Emily's lessons; you'd have to improve your reading and writing," he said, and leafed through the papers on his desk.

Henry realized that these could only be reports on him — school reports, psychologists' reports. And his heart sank.

Reverend Oswald stood up, walked toward him, and patted him lightly on the shoulder, like he was indicating that the interview was over.

"You don't have to be ashamed of your stutter, Henry. I have been told that singing can cure a stutter. Have you heard that?"

Henry stood up slowly, shaking his head.

"Reading out loud and singing too; that should do the trick," the reverend said, like the problem had already been solved.

Emily appeared in the hall and asked Henry to follow her into the kitchen. She poured him a cup of coffee, and he sat on the chair by the stove and wrapped his trembling fingers around the coffee mug, the sweat turning cold on his back.

She said something about how she had worried about him when he hadn't shown up for dinner, how much she wanted him to tell her if he was feeling bad, how she longed for him to be happy.

Then she handed him a small book.

"I'd like you to have this," she said.

Henry glanced at the book in his hand. It had a silly drawing of a little boy on the cover, standing on a ball or a planet or something.

"It's a beautiful story; once you start you can't put it down, I promise you," she said in a happy tone of voice.

Holding the book made Henry's stomach churn instantly. They hadn't let him go without punishment, after all. He hadn't been set free. No, not at all. He had been handed the worst sentence he could've imagined.

For the first time, Henry dared to look straight into Emily's eyes for a brief moment, pleading for her to change her mind about this.

"I'd like you to read a little every day," she said, smiling. "And maybe you can come over when I'm in the kitchen and we can talk about the story," she added, and left the kitchen.

If only the reverend had locked him in the Boiler Room or made him rebuild the Cairn of Christ. Anything but this; anything but a book.

7.
Things Lost and Things Found

Without him realizing it, Henry's life had found a new rhythm. His daily routine had become so familiar that it was as if he'd been here for years. He had felt secure in his routine; milking every morning and evening, feeding the cows and the sheep, shoveling the cow dung. He had even learned to endure the sermons and the religious lessons, although with some difficulty.

And the boys never bothered him. They were afraid of him; they thought he was retarded, maybe a dangerous criminal even. Sometimes they shouted rude remarks from a safe distance, calling him names and such. But that was nothing. He didn't care. He had his work, his routine, and the occasional moment of bliss, sitting in silence beside the warm stove, with a coffee mug in his hands, while Emily cooked rye pancakes.

But now everything had been ruined because of the book.

It was like a threatening shadow creeping up behind him every day, everywhere he went. It ruined the pleasure of tending to the cows, milking them, brushing their hides clean. He fumbled clumsily around with his hands while milking, forgetting to grease the udders, pulling too hard on their teats so the cows bellowed in pain and kicked their hind legs, sometimes hitting the bucket so the milk flowed into the dung canal. Not even wrestling with Noah could ease the gnawing anxiety punching his stomach from the inside.

When he'd gotten to his room that day, he had thrown the book to the floor and kicked it so it flew right under the chest of drawers. He was determined to let it lie there forever.

But he knew that soon Emily would start to ask him about the story, like she had said. If he told her he had lost the book, she might just give him a new one. She might call on him to attend her lessons and order him to read. Then all the boys would know that he was no threat, he was not dangerous, he was just a stupid cripple who couldn't read, a stuttering retard.

They would laugh, they would make jokes about him, and then they would begin to hate him instead of fearing him. Then they would plan to corner him somewhere, perhaps in the barn, and beat him up.

Each morning at breakfast he became more and more uneasy. He felt he could sense their anger toward him, as if they already knew. Oh, yes, they knew, he was certain. Weren't Paul and Timothy glancing toward him and then looking at each other, nodding, as if agreeing on something? They were making their plans, that was obvious. And the others, who had hardly seemed to notice him before; now they turned in their seats in Sunday sermons when he entered the garage and gave him a hard look. He had heard some of them behind the barn, right under the window of his room, whispering, giggling. But when he'd limped around the corner as fast as he could, holding the shovel with both hands, ready to strike, they were gone. He heard laughter far off, wicked laughter.

The pretty boys were plotting against him once more.

He couldn't tell Emily, for there was nothing to tell, except for his suspicions, and they were far too complicated to put into words. Besides, she was pushing him toward the inevitable: she was going to make him read out loud. There was no way he could expect any help from her.

She had been kind, and maybe she didn't mean any harm; she was just following the reverend's orders. Why did she do that? Why was she even married to that man? How could such a lovely woman be under the heel of such an awful man, such an angry, screaming madman?

Perhaps he had forced Emily to stay with him somehow. Perhaps he had something on her, or he had brainwashed her or—and Henry shuddered to think of it—perhaps he beat her up.

Yes, that's why she didn't dare leave, because Oswald would chase her, drag her back, and beat her up. Henry had seen it happen before with his mom, years ago, when they'd lived with this horrible man; he'd locked Henry in a closet while he beat up his mom. No matter how he'd tried to cover his ears, Henry had heard. The screams and the curses and the sound of hard knuckles hitting soft flesh were engraved on his memory.

So that's why Emily is stuck here, in her own hell, with that terrible man tormenting her, Henry thought. That scratch on her chin, the other day . . . Had he punched her in the face? Of course the bastard was clever enough to beat her so nobody would notice. Perhaps she was all bruised under her shirt, perhaps she stayed up all night, sobbing quietly into her pillow, praying to God for some kind of rescue.

And what of God? Why did he allow all this to happen?

Of course! Henry clenched his fists and spat in the dung canal: Of course God is on the reverend's side. After all, the reverend is his man, right?

Now that Henry had realized the truth, now that the veil of falsehood and lies had been lifted from his eyes, he was fuming with rage. He limped back and forth on the edge of the dung canal, cursing through his teeth. How blind he had been, how utterly blind and stupid. That damned priest was going to get what he deserved. Oh, yes; somehow, Henry was going to make him pay.

Suddenly he remembered the book and froze in his tracks.

In an instant he knew exactly what to do.

The fresh ocean breeze blew harder as he got closer to the Gallows. He limped down Spine Break Path as fast as his clubfoot allowed, breathing hard, with a sweet feeling of vengeance in his angry heart at going against the reverend's orders.

Standing finally on the edge, almost out of breath, drying his nose on the sleeve of his sweater, he gazed over the vast ocean.

Along the cliffs, the waves plunged through cracks and caves, exploding up through blowholes, gushing high into the air. The water fell around him in heavy drops, hitting the black lava slabs with loud smacks. The birds screeched in the air around him and below him, maybe bidding him welcome again; maybe telling him to be careful on the slippery edge. For a second he could see himself falling through the air, arms outstretched like wings, before he plunged into the roaring waves.

But this was not the day to give in and surrender. No. Today he was going to fight back.

He picked up a small rock and pulled the book from under his sweater. He put the rock between the pages and rolled the book around it. Then he threw it as hard as he could. The cover folded out like wings, pages turning, flapping in the wind, soaring through the air, falling, falling, until the book was engulfed by an approaching wave and drowned in white foam.

Henry couldn't help but laugh. *Let them give me their books!* he thought. *I know exactly where to put them!*

He lay down like the first time, feeling the rock underneath him tremble against his heart. And he felt again the sensation of becoming one with the cold cliffs, his heart beating in rhythm with the pounding waves. He lay still for a long time until he noticed that the tide was receding.

Little by little, the surf calmed down as the mighty ocean drew its breath ever more slowly. The surface became soft and tempting, like a warm duvet; the ocean whispered and hummed, breathing gently, almost like it had fallen asleep.

The wreck of *Young Hope* was stuck tightly on its side between two rocks that now became visible, covered in longhaired seaweed that moved lazily to and fro on the slow waves. The hollow sound of the waves echoed through the rift in the hull, their force slapping its rusty insides, bending the iron bars that stuck out like ribs on a half-rotten carcass. Right underneath him, a sandbank appeared far below, following the curve of the bay.

Henry's heart had become calm, his head was empty; his rage had subsided like the furious waves.

A little farther along the edge, he noticed a rusty iron bar, which had been drilled into the cliff. He moved carefully closer on his stomach.

There was a long rusty chain fastened to the iron bar, which ran over the edge and down the steep cliff face. Stretching his neck a little farther, Henry saw that steps had been chiseled here and there into the steep cliff wall, winding along the chain, all the way down to the sandbank far below.

Who would want to go down there? he thought. *And why?*

Then he remembered Emily's story about the Miracle Man, who had rescued the sailors of the trawler, the one who had rowed his little boat from these very shores, without anyone understanding how he had managed to put the boat to sea or pull it back up on the edge.

It took Henry a long time to gather enough courage to try and climb down. It was difficult because of his leg; it slipped from underneath him on the wet rocks. He tightened his grip on the rusty chain, his heart beating faster than ever. When he looked down, it seemed so much farther now than when he was up on the edge.

Gusts of wind pushed him around on the chain or pulled at him, so he tightened his grip and pressed his forehead against the cliff, his legs dangling in the air.

Midway down he came to a ledge that protruded from the cliff wall. He let the chain go and sat down to rest.

Drying his nose on his sleeve, he shivered with excitement, sitting alone in the middle of a steep cliff face, surrounded by the white birds hurling themselves into the void. He shivered with excitement and fear, but it was a good fear. He wondered about the Miracle Man; how had he moved the boat up and down the cliff face? And what had become of the boat? It was a puzzle. And he was going to solve it.

The chain was obviously meant for holding on to while climbing up or down, but it looked like there was something missing. While pondering this he noticed that behind him was an opening in the cliff.

It was a cave.

Its mouth was curved and the floor smooth. The ceiling was low and covered in tiny drops and needles, frozen forever in stone. Pulling himself inside, Henry saw that the cave was deep enough to give shelter if it rained, but not high enough to stand upright in. A strange thing happened when he sat down inside. The sounds of the ocean were somehow magnified in there. Its humming voice echoed in the dome of the cave, surrounding him completely. It was as if he became one with the ocean, and the land didn't exist anymore; nobody existed but him and the almighty ocean.

As the tide came in, the surf began to roar below, hurling

itself at the cliffs, shooting foam all the way up onto the ledge. The powerful rumble engulfed him, echoing around him, inside him. He was alone in the world and nobody could hear him now.

Without fear or shame he raised his rusty voice and sang with the ocean, intoning the wordless poem of the rising and falling surf, all day long until his throat hurt and his voice was almost gone.

8.

The Prince of Thieves

"Where is it? Where's the book?" she asked, standing in the middle of his room, looking around her. He had finished the morning milking, and Emily had arrived to change his bedsheets and bring him clean clothes. He didn't have an answer ready; he'd forgotten all about the book and hadn't thought of a lie to tell her.

"I l-lost it," he stuttered.

Emily sighed, obviously disappointed and a little annoyed.

"Oh, that's a shame," she said. "That's a real shame. It's the only copy I have, and it's my favorite."

Henry was in a hurry; it was the day of the week that the milk tanker arrived, and he had to lift the heavy containers full of milk out of the cooling tank, drag them outside, and then lift them up onto the platform on the tanker.

"Sorry," he murmured, wanting to turn away.

"Do try to find it, Henry dear, would you? It would really mean a lot to me to get it back."

"Yes," he breathed, and turned in the doorway.

"It's almost spring, and some of the boys will be leaving soon," she said as she folded his duvet neatly.

Henry waited in the doorway, sidestepping between hope and fear.

"And two new boys will be arriving, both your age," she said, and picked up the dirty bedsheets from the floor, rolling them into a ball in her arms.

"There'll be a lot of work this summer, so we'll just hold off on the reading until autumn, all right?"

She walked past him with her arms full of dirty linen. He breathed in the soft fragrance that trailed behind her, of white soap and purple flowers and the warm sun in a clear blue sky. And his heart jumped with relief.

When he lifted the milk containers out of the cooling tank they felt light as feathers, and he carried them outside with no effort at all. When the tanker arrived he grabbed the containers by the handle with one hand, placed the other hand under the bottom, and almost threw them up in the air. The driver stood on a platform, ready to pull up the containers, but he was quite unprepared for having to grab them in midair.

"Whoa! Not so fast," he cried. "Feeling strong today, are we?" He grinned.

Henry couldn't help but smile.

"Yeah," he growled. "Very strong."

Early spring was the most exciting time for the little ones.

They were happily captivated by the wonder of the little lambs that were being born into the world. Emily had put them on night shifts, two at a time, and if any ewes started to give birth in the middle of the night, one of them was to run to the house and wake her.

Reverend Oswald used the opportunity to talk a lot about the Lamb of God. The boys had seldom understood his preaching so well.

At breakfast they had sleepless, bloodshot eyes from staying awake and watching over the ewes. They had a competition among them over who had delivered the most lambs. Henry didn't understand their excitement, how they marveled at the fragile state of a newborn lamb barely able to rise on its trembling feet.

He wasn't put on any night shifts in the lambing season, for he had the cows to take care of, and he fed the sheep twice a day too. He was disgusted by the slimy bugs that the ewes squeezed out of their rears. They woke him up, abruptly, in the middle of the night with their high-pitched bleating, so he had to cover his ears with his arms. And to make matters worse, the bitter stench of sheep shit oozed through the wall, somehow stronger than before.

Finally all the ewes had given birth, and the old farmhand, who now lived on a neighboring farm, came to inspect them.

Henry heard that the boys had nicknamed him the Brute, because of his manners, bulk, and filthy language. He was a tall, tanned man with a cigarette constantly hanging from the corner of his wide mouth, wearing blue overalls that were far too baggy for him, spotted with everything from paint to plain dirt.

The Brute had arrived to brand the lambs.

About half the boys were in the dormitory, packing their bags, for they were leaving on the afternoon bus. Some were going back home, others to new foster parents in another part of the country.

The rest of the boys sat in a row upon the fence inside the sheep shed, unaware of the horror that was about to take place. Henry stood by the door that opened into the barn and watched.

The Brute moved quickly, seizing a lamb in his large hands, kneeling on the slatted floor, holding the trembling animal in his crotch with one hand and brandishing a pair of rusty shears in the other, stroking the white velvet ear with its sharp blade. Then he glanced at the boys on the fence with a murky grin.

"Now I'll teach you how to do this," he said. "The brand mark for this farm is: tip-cut left; slant-cut right. Now, how am I to do that?"

The boys had no idea what he was talking about.

The Brute held the lamb tightly, placing the velvet ear between the rusty blades of the shears, cutting the tip of the left ear in a quick move.

The lamb jumped up, screaming, shaking its head wildly, as the blood ran down its curly cheeks. Its mother bleated loudly on the other side of the fence, furiously trying to climb over to protect her little one. The boys' faces turned pale. Some covered their ears because of the lamb's high-pitched screams of pain. Or perhaps they just felt for the little thing, rubbing their own ears to try to soothe those of the lamb.

The Brute grinned and squinted through the cigarette smoke, assessing the boys.

"Here," he said, pointing the shears to one of the boys. "You'll do the other ear."

But the boy shook his head. The Brute shrugged, dug his strong fingers into the curly wool, held the lamb firmly between his thighs, and made a slant-cut to the right ear of the screaming little lamb. Then he ordered the boys to bring him another lamb.

"And keep them coming," he growled. "We haven't got all day."

That afternoon, when all the lambs had been branded this way, the Brute told the boys to herd the flock toward the low mountains in the north. The lambs ran beside their mothers, red blood on their thin little necks, crying with their soft, bright voices.

Henry stayed in the yard and watched the flock go up the road. As they crossed, he saw the bus appear. It had to stop and wait while the sheep crossed, but then it turned toward the farm and eased across the yard, the large wheels crunching the gravel.

Reverend Oswald and Emily were saying farewell to the boys who were leaving. Henry wondered if any of them would return in the autumn, perhaps a little harder in the face, their eyes a little colder.

All of them shook hands with the reverend, but when they turned to Emily she embraced them tightly and they started to cry. Emily was having a hard time saying good-bye as well, Henry noticed, wiping tears from her eyes.

When the bus finally drove off, Henry saw a tall, thin boy standing alone in the yard. He spat through his teeth and threw back his long black hair with a sudden jerk of the head. His thumbs were hooked in the pockets of his tight jeans, and he looked around with an arrogant air.

Emily and the reverend approached him, but Henry noticed that when the reverend offered him his hand, the boy didn't take it. Emily took the reverend aside and they talked for a while in low voices.

Henry sat on the Cairn of Christ and watched the boy. He seemed to be about the same age as himself, but he was handsome. His face was lean, with a strong jaw, straight nose, thick black eyebrows, and long shiny black hair. He stood, relaxed, right next to his duffel bag, like he didn't care about a thing in the world, dressed in a thin T-shirt and a short, worn leather jacket, and old cowboy boots.

There was something about him that made Henry curious, perhaps his boldness at refusing to shake hands with the reverend. If only Henry knew the words to start a conversation with him. If only he could somehow show him that they were perhaps of the same mind, that he too wanted nothing more than to give the reverend as much hell as possible, that perhaps the two of them could find a way to make it happen, that the two of them could, perhaps, become friends.

He felt a strong urge to make the boy notice him, so he might, somehow, indicate to him that he wasn't just an ugly cripple, but someone to be respected, a person with serious responsibilities on the farm, and therefore someone to rely on, to trust.

He had no idea how to put his thoughts into words, and since the boy didn't even seem to notice him sitting there, Henry began to worry that in a short while Emily would take the boy inside, and he would miss his chance.

Finally he cleared his throat loudly and spat on the gravel.

But the boy didn't turn around to look. He just stood there, waiting, as if he hadn't heard a thing.

Emily and the reverend finished their conversation, and Emily walked to the house. The reverend told the boy sternly to follow him. The boy picked up his duffel bag and walked behind the reverend toward the dormitory in the old sheep shed. Henry didn't see him at dinner and wondered if the reverend had locked him up already for refusing to shake hands with him.

Early next morning, the boys crowded around the breakfast table as Emily introduced the new boy.

"This is John," she said. "Our new farmhand. You will show him respect and courtesy."

"Welcome, John," said Reverend Oswald, and the boys murmured: "Welcome, John!"

Then everybody sat down, clasped their hands, and bowed

their heads. Except for John. He glanced over the table, his eyes a shimmering green, a faint hint of mockery on his lips. Reverend Oswald had hardly begun the prayer when John stretched out his arm and started to scoop porridge into his bowl. The reverend fell silent and looked up. Everyone froze. John continued like nothing had happened, poured milk over the porridge, and began to eat.

"There are rules here, which you will have to follow like everyone else," the reverend said. "Put that spoon down."

"But I'm hungry," John replied.

"We're all hungry, John," the reverend said. "But before eating, we give our thanks to God."

"I don't believe in God," John said dryly, and continued eating.

There was a moment of silence, and the little boys sank in their seats. Finally the reverend spoke, obviously trying hard to restrain his anger.

"But we do. So perhaps you would be so kind as to show us some respect and courtesy by not eating while we pray."

The words were polite enough, but the tone of his voice was not. John shrugged and put the spoon in his bowl with a loud clank.

"Sure," he said, and leaned back in his chair, smiling, folding his arms on his chest.

Reverend Oswald began the prayer again, his voice trembling a little.

Henry felt a surge of joy; finally here was someone brave enough to challenge the reverend. Finally! Henry couldn't wait for the chance to talk to John, to let him know that they could be in this together, that he wasn't on the reverend's side, but on John's side.

But he had to be careful so the reverend wouldn't suspect anything. And Henry had to choose his words carefully, form a clear sentence in his mind before speaking to John. If he started to stutter or forget what he wanted to say, then John might think he was a retard after all, a stupid, worthless cripple.

But the days went by and Henry never found a chance to approach John. He continued to behave stubbornly at breakfast, lunch, and dinner; he even stormed out of the garage in the middle of a Sunday service. The reverend stopped the service and followed him outside. While Emily, Henry, and the rest of the boys sat quietly inside the garage, the two of them had a heated argument out in the yard. The reverend came back alone, said a short prayer, and then left, while Emily played the organ and the boys sang.

For a whole week John was nowhere to be seen: he had been locked up in the Boiler Room.

When he appeared again at breakfast he was pale in the face and his green eyes didn't shimmer anymore. Now he clasped his hands like everyone else and murmured "Amen" after the reverend's prayer. Henry knew the power of the reverend's words. He could well imagine that their influence was even stronger when one was locked up in a small room while the reverend gave thundering speeches, demanding that one should say one's prayers out loud, the prayers that the reverend had ordered one to learn by heart. John looked tired and worn out. The reverend, on the other hand, had regained his confidence as well as his oratory skills, beaming with energy and power at the head of the table.

That morning, the Brute arrived after breakfast, for the day had come to clean out the sheep sheds. The reverend and the Brute had a short conversation in the yard before the reverend got in his car, an old yellow Volvo with freckles of rust on the paint. The Volvo disappeared in a cloud of dust on the road, and the Brute took John with him to the sheep sheds.

Henry stood in the doorway, which opened into the barn, and watched as they picked up the slatted floorboards and dragged them out into the yard, where the little ones took over and began to scrape them clean.

Below the boards, the cistern was full to the brim with coal-black, tightly packed manure. The stench was bitter and awful. The Brute stood on the firm slab with a cigarette in his mouth and a sharp shovel in his hands. He cut one clod of manure and threw it in the wheelbarrow.

"There," he said, and handed the shovel to John. "Keep doing that till there's no shit left in there. And when that's done, there's the other shed to be cleaned out."

Then he walked out and drove away in his red pickup in a cloud of dust.

John cut one clod after the other until he had filled the wheelbarrow. Then he pushed it over the threshold across a plank and emptied it on the heap behind the barn. When he came back inside, he glanced at Henry in the doorway but said nothing.

John was already sweating, the back of his T-shirt drenched. Suddenly he turned around and gave Henry a sharp look and thrust his chin forward.

"What do you want?" he asked brusquely.

For a brief moment Henry was dumbstruck, for he hadn't decided on his words, hadn't found a way to say the things he wanted to say. So he said nothing, kept his mouth firmly shut, but his mind was spinning like mad, searching for the right words, for this was an important moment. And he knew he had to seize it.

"Are you deaf?"

Henry shook his head.

"You live in the cowshed, right?"

Henry nodded. He almost smiled. But he knew how his smile could be misunderstood as a mocking scowl, so he held back and bit on his lip.

"Then you're lost," John said. "These are the sheep sheds."

He continued to shovel the shit and chuck the large chunks into the wheelbarrow.

Henry felt that this was a beginning of a conversation, of a kind. If he could only come up with some reply, something easy, then John might perhaps continue talking, and he would have time to think of something else. The most important thing was to say something, anything, and not let the silence draw on for too long.

Then suddenly he had an amusing thought. But how to put it into words, so John would understand the joke, was another matter.

"I fed them," he said.

John looked up. "You fed who?"

Henry pointed with his chin at the empty sheep shed. "Them," he said.

John looked at him pensively for a moment with his green eyes, perhaps wondering if he was retarded. Then he smirked and threw back his long black hair with a quick jerk.

"Feed them less next time," he said, and kept on working.

Henry stood still in the doorway and couldn't help but smile. John had actually understood the joke. He couldn't think of anything else to say, so he just stood there for a while, with his hands deep in his pockets, a broad grin on his face.

Somehow the sheep shit didn't stink nearly as bad as before.

He couldn't fall asleep that night, wondering how his life would have turned out if he'd been like John. How easily he would have laughed off every opponent, how lightly he would have taken every insult, like it was nothing at all; how he would have enjoyed being the cool guy, shooting out short, sharp sentences that would make everyone gasp with admiration or shut up for good. How sweet to have been admired by the pretty boys, loved by the girls. How different everything would have been.

He lay still for a long time, staring into the darkness around him, stroking his thick short fingers lightly across his ugly face.

He was no John, and he never would be. But perhaps John

might become a friend. If only he could find a way to make that happen. How happy he would be, having a friend like John. Just thinking about it made him feel good, made him feel strong, worthy.

Right before he fell asleep he wondered why John had been sent to this place. Was he a criminal of some sort, a thief perhaps? He could imagine John as a Prince of Thieves. And he was relieved that the week in the Boiler Room had not broken John's spirit: he had obviously just decided to play along, feign obedience to avoid further punishment.

Henry smiled in the darkness, firmly resolved to try again to make contact with John as soon as possible. After all, today had not been that bad; he had made a joke, and John had understood it.

In his whole life, that had never happened before.

9.

The Reverend's Holy Project

It was a sunny day with a warm breeze coming in from the south, and the time had come to put the cows out to pasture. They had been growing more irritable with each day and wouldn't lie down in their stalls. Their moos had acquired a different tone, agitated, impatient, demanding. They sniffed the air, breathed heavily, and frowned.

Noah, on the other hand, had become sadder with each day, resting his head on the stall fence, rolling his eyes, whimpering like a puppy.

After breakfast Emily had told the little ones with an excited smile that today would be great fun, but the boys froze with terror. Their love of the little lambs was directly proportionate to their terror of the big cows. They couldn't understand why they had to be set free. Some ran straight to their rooms and locked the doors. Others stood tight together on a cart, trembling with fear and excitement.

Henry limped from stall to stall and untied the cows' collars one by one and watched as they stumbled to the door, toward the bright sunlight outside.

Old Red, usually so calm, composed, and gentle, was the first to go. Her legs trembled as she staggered impatiently toward the door. She hesitated for a moment, expanding her nostrils and shuddering. Then she mooed and jumped over the threshold. One foot touched the soil, and the wet mud pressed up through her cloven hoof. It was as if the heavy burden of the long winter had rested on that one leg. She pulled it free from the mud with a long-drawn sucking sound—and summer had arrived.

Old Red rushed out of the door, heaving heavily, with gawking eyes, her ears pricked up, saliva dripping from her mouth. She mooed again, galloped forward, raised her tail high in the air, and a fountain of shit streamed out, dotting her course.

The others followed: Little Gray, Spotty with her large horns, Brandy and Belle, Jenny, Maggy, and Nelly. They all ran in surprised excitement, bumping into everything in their path, thrusting their backsides into the air, mooing and shitting. It was like watching a silly cartoon.

Then, finally, the little ones laughed.

But inside the dark cowshed, Noah kicked the fence and grumbled.

Henry was scraping the shit off the stalls when John entered and looked around him. Outside, the cows were running wild and the boys screamed.

"Why does he have to stay in?" John asked.

Henry didn't reply straightaway, because he didn't want to stutter. He became a little shy, but also happy that John had entered his little world, the cowshed, to have a talk. And he didn't seem to be in any hurry, but waited patiently while Henry gathered his thoughts.

"He would kill," he finally replied.

John nodded and glanced at the bull. "Where do the cows go to pasture?" he asked.

"East," Henry said.

"East? Where's east?"

"That way," Henry said, pointing with the shovel.

"And north?" John asked. "Which way is that?"

"That way," Henry replied after a while, pointing at the wall.

Then John asked no more questions, but simply nodded and walked out.

Henry fetched a whip that hung on a nail above the door, made from the broken wooden handle of a rake with a black nylon string attached to it. Wiping off dust and grime, he swung it in the air and cracked it at the floor a few times, just for fun. He had spoken with John, and it hadn't been that difficult; no, not at all.

When Henry left the cowshed, Noah growled and banged his head against the fence in protest. Emily had given him directions where to herd the cows but told him not to worry; they'd know the way, she'd said.

The cows had finished their happy running around and stood panting at the gate. Old Red had calmed herself and rolled her tongue around the fresh green straws by the roadside. She led the group through the gate, and the others pushed behind her, rolling their eyes and butting one another in the belly from sheer happiness.

Little by little, the group found its easy pace, following the old path beside the road, breathing in the scent of summer. They nodded their heavy heads in a steady rhythm, pricking up their ears when a bird chirped close by and sniffing the fresh streams that trickled down the low hills.

Henry limped behind, thinking about John, who had spoken to him like he was a normal person. He felt good to have answered back correctly. It also felt good to know something that John didn't know; he had asked Henry the question as if it was a secret they shared between them, Henry and John.

He led the cows by the path that lay between the road and the mountainside, all the way until he was past the slopes with the red pumice gravel, where a small valley opened up inside the fence-enclosed pasture, just as Emily had described that morning.

Limping back to the farm, Henry listened to the grass move in a green whisper. He breathed in the soft fragrance of the tiny flowers nodding their heads in the warm breeze, watched a bee moving lazily from one to the next, while the birds sang and chirped all over the lava field.

It was a beautiful day indeed, and a happy one too.

Reverend Oswald stood in the middle of the yard, with John and the boys all around him. When Henry came closer he heard the reverend say that this would be a summer they would never forget, for this summer they would build a church together, dedicated to Jesus Christ our Savior.

"And all you boys will lend a hand," he said, smiling down at the eager faces of the young boys. "And when you're all grown up, you will take your children for a Sunday ride, show them the church, and say: I built this church with my brothers at the Home of Lesser Brethren; together we laid the foundations for Jesus Christ's new church."

The boys chuckled and sniggered, but the reverend was in a good mood and just clapped his hands and shouted, "Follow me!"

Then he marched ahead of the boys toward a grassy knoll in the lava, a little west of the farmhouses, and Henry followed.

When they'd all gathered around him he said: "Our good neighbor will be arriving in a little while with lots of shovels, and you'll start digging right here." He pointed at four markers, nailed in the ground, that marked out the foundations.

"For like the good Lord said, 'A wise man doesn't build his house upon the sand.' We must shovel the sand away until we reach the bedrock underneath; the bedrock, which is Jesus Christ himself.

"Out there," he continued, and pointed farther west, "is a big fine slab of smooth lava. We'll break that slab into stones for the foundation. Then we'll pile the stones on the bedrock, for the stones are like those who stand together with Jesus

Christ. And from that foundation, his temple of victory will rise, the house of God himself."

The boys stood silent in the breeze, not sure if they had understood him completely. But one thing was certain; there was going to be lots of hard work. The good news was that there wouldn't be any classes for weeks to come.

"Thank God," a few whispered.

But John frowned and shook his head. Reverend Oswald looked at him sternly.

"Would you like to say something, John?"

"Yeah," John replied, and threw his hair back. "Is this a slave camp or what? I'm not sure it's legal for you to use us like workers here."

Oswald's eyes became cold, and his sincere joy vanished into thin air.

"Not legal? What would you know about the law?"

"I'm just saying," John said, "that it doesn't feel right."

"If I read your report correctly," Oswald began with a sly grin playing on his lips, "I recall that the reason you are here is because you broke the law. And so whatever you 'feel' might be right or wrong is unlikely to stand up in any court."

"That doesn't make me your slave," John shot back at him.

The boys stood absolutely still, not daring to move a muscle. Only their frightened eyes moved, glancing at one another.

"What you call slavery, my boy, is what normal people consider healthy work. But of course you wouldn't know much about that, now, would you?" Oswald said with a wicked smile.

The little boys chuckled shyly, but John looked around him, annoyed that he didn't have the support of the others.

"Are you going to let these little boys slave away with a shovel and a crowbar?" John said.

But now Reverend Oswald had regained his bearings and broke him off with full force. "This is the devil speaking!" he shouted, and pointed an accusing finger at John. "The devil is speaking through his obedient servant, to mock and belittle the great work that awaits us here: to build a church in the name of Jesus Christ!"

He turned to the boys and gathered them around him, like a mother goose herding her chicks to safety under her wings.

"Look at him, all of you; look at the devil before you—there you see him. This is what he looks like. This is what he sounds like when he's bent on destroying the good work of the Lord. Aye! Planting seeds of doubt and suspicion, calling the healthy work of love and humility for the Lord 'slavery'! How cunningly he turns everything upside down. Look at him! This is the beast that we're fighting!"

The boys were stunned. But John's face was empty of all emotion, as if he didn't believe his own ears.

"Are you joking?" he said. "I'm only saying that this is no job for little boys."

"So, now you're the liberating angel of innocent children, are you?" Oswald said, laughing. "That's the devil's way all right: constantly changing his shape, trying everything to make you trust his sincerity."

Then he raised his fist in the air, shouting, "Be gone, Satan! Be gone, you father of lies, for our souls belong to Jesus Christ, the son of the living God!"

Henry turned as he heard the Brute's pickup approach. The shovels rattled back and forth in the back of the truck with a clashing noise, sounding like a thousand church bells ringing at once as it toiled across the rugged lava toward the knoll.

The Brute distributed the shovels among the boys, but Reverend Oswald had a quiet word with him and pointed at John. Then the reverend turned to Henry.

"You don't have to be here, Henry, you have enough to do already, although you're welcome to join in, whenever you can."

Henry just nodded and turned away, but the reverend hadn't finished.

"Wait a bit," he said. "I want you to do me a favor; go to the smithy and find a crowbar and a sledgehammer. They're supposed to be there; they're for John." He glanced at John, who stood there, listening.

"John will be the foreman in the rock mine," the reverend added, "for that's no job for a little boy; that's a job for a strong man."

The mockery in his voice was laid on so thick that even Henry couldn't help but notice. The Brute grinned with a cigarette hanging from the corner of his mouth. John frowned and spat, but said nothing.

Henry had never been inside the smithy before. It had been the realm of the little boys, their playhouse on rainy days, their source of timber and tools for the little huts they'd been building outside.

The smithy was like three sheds that had been thrust together. In the middle was the working area. On the walls were endless rows of shelves, filled with all kinds of tools, nail packs, screws of various sizes, old radios, motor parts. Most of it was covered in greasy dust, as if it hadn't been touched for ages.

There was a heap of tools on the floor, hammers and saws, a pack of nails around a boxcar that the boys were making; tires made of wood with cuts of rubber from real tires fastened with nails.

But the crowbar and sledgehammer were nowhere to be seen.

He felt bad having been sent on this errand. John might think he was on the reverend's side, after all. But right now there was nothing he could do about it.

At one end were stacks of timber, full of nails and encrusted with hardened concrete. At the other end were things that obviously hadn't been moved around for a long time. There was old furniture stacked up under a plastic cover that was damp and moldy. But in a corner, behind the stack, he thought he saw the handle of a sledgehammer, or some other tool, right next to three wooden barrels.

He eased himself past the stack of furniture and began to move the barrels away. They were full of tangled fishing nets. Bits of old seaweed still clung to the nets, crisp and dry as a cracker so it crumbled into dust between his fingers when he touched it.

When the barrels were out of the way he saw a rusty iron wheel on the floor, with a long steel cable wrapped around it. The wheel was quite heavy, and it took some effort to move it to the side. Then, finally, he saw the crowbar and the heavy sledgehammer that the reverend had mentioned.

There were two oars as well, standing in the corner.

Henry was about to pick up the tools when his leg brushed against something that was covered with green sailcloth. He stepped back, dragging the tools with him, and pulled at the sailcloth. It fell to the floor and suddenly the blood rushed to his cheeks.

He gasped, and the crowbar fell to the floor with a loud clang.

From under the sailcloth a boat appeared, a small white rowboat.

He moved closer, touching it gently with his fingertips. The dust twisted and turned in the air, catching the light from the bright sunbeams pouring through the window, causing the boat to glow in a heavenly light.

Two panels divided the space inside it into three compartments. In the middle one was a fishing line with rusty hooks, rifle shells, and the desiccated corpse of a seagull with empty eye sockets, its beak wide open.

Henry stood for a long time, with flushed cheeks and gleaming eyes. He had discovered the Miracle Man's rowboat, the very one he had mysteriously managed to move down the steep sea cliffs without anyone understanding how.

His mind was moving fast now, like a bird soaring through the air, catching the ocean breeze under its wings, shooting onward, out of sight.

He glanced at the iron wheel on the floor.

Through the middle of the wheel was a square hole, as if the wheel was supposed to be fastened to a square-shaped iron bar.

Henry knew instantly where that iron bar was located, for he had discovered it himself the day he'd gotten rid of the book, the day he'd climbed down the chain and found the cave.

His eyes moved from the wheel to the boat and back again. He could see how the Miracle Man had done it. Henry had solved the riddle, he alone and nobody else.

He couldn't help but laugh out loud.

Right after dinner, Henry carried the container with the milk for the house inside to the kitchen. There were ten empty bottles on the kitchen table, which had to be filled and stored in the refrigerator. The container had a tap near the bottom, so Henry put it up on a chair, turned the tap, and filled the bottles one by one.

His mind was occupied with his discovery; he was wondering if he had covered the boat well enough so the little boys wouldn't find it. This was a most important secret that he would keep to himself, unless, of course, John became his friend. This was the kind of secret to share only with a trusted friend. Still, John's friendship was only a hope; how to make it happen remained a puzzle.

He was still trying to come up with a plan of how he could approach John the next day, when he heard voices in the dining room.

He had thought Emily and the reverend were in the living room, as they usually were in the evenings, when he realized they were still in the dining room, next to the kitchen. Perhaps they'd been talking since he came in, but he hadn't noticed. He did now though, for Emily was raising her voice.

"I can't accept this," he heard her say. "You sold the sheep without even discussing it with me?"

"It had to be done," he said. "With so many of the boys gone, the grant from the state has been cut. And we have a church to build."

"What's wrong with the garage?" she asked. "It's served us well for almost ten years now. Why suddenly build a church?"

"We've discussed this before, Emily. You know the people here. They won't come to mass in the garage. But if we had a proper country church, they would feel differently," he said.

"Oh no, they won't," she sighed. "Even *their* reverend is preaching to half-empty pews on Sundays, so why on earth would they come to us? And what of the cows?" she asked. "Are you going to sell them too, when the money runs out?"

"We could manage with fewer cows," he replied. "Then we could also rent out the other field. We could at least sell the bull."

Henry's heart jumped in his chest. He almost dropped a full bottle of milk on the floor. He put it carefully on the table and moved quietly toward the dining-room door, leaning against it, listening.

"The cows won't give any milk," Emily said. "Not if they don't have a bull when they're cycling."

"Cycling?" the reverend asked. "What are you talking about?"

"When they're in heat and want a calf," she answered. "When they're in need of sperm," she added. "They'll go sterile."

"I see," he murmured, and cleared his throat. "Then maybe we'll sell them too."

"Why live on a farm if there are no animals?" she asked, her voice almost breaking. "Why did we decide to have a home for young boys on a farm? Have you seen the happiness in their eyes in the lambing season? Have you noticed Henry's improvement, now that he has a responsibility, a regular routine to live by, caring for the cows? That's the reason we came here, Oswald; to give young boys a home, teach them how to care for animals, so they would learn new values; to give them a chance. A better chance than their parents had."

"We can have a few sheep on loan from our neighbor next spring, if you like," he said. "Then the boys can experience the lambing season."

"You're missing the point," she said. "These boys need love and affection, they need to win small victories every day so they'll begin to believe in themselves; they need tasks to solve to make them proud. This is what our home is all about. Isn't the boys' happiness more important than some stupid building?"

Henry had never imagined that Emily could be capable of such anger. But she was, and Henry was angry now too. He wanted to burst in and punch the reverend in the face.

"It is a church for Jesus Christ," the reverend said sternly.

"And what was it that Jesus once said?" she snapped. "'Whatever you did for even the least of my brothers, you did for me.' Do you think he was talking about love or architecture?"

There was a long silence before the reverend finally spoke.

"You don't understand me," he said. "You never have."

Henry heard a door slamming shut. There was a moment of silence. Then he heard footsteps on the gravel outside. A car engine roared and then drove off. The sound of the engine lingered on in the quiet of the evening until it finally disappeared.

Henry opened the door quietly and peeked into the dining room.

Emily sat on a chair, her back to the door, her auburn hair flowing, bathed in soft orange light from a wall lamp. She was hiding her face in her hands; her shoulders were trembling.

Henry felt his throat tighten, his eyes sting. How he longed to comfort her, dry her tears and tell her that everything would be all right, that he was on her side, that he would fight for her, fight with her, that together they would stand firm against the reverend.

But he couldn't move. He swallowed the lump in his throat, clenched his fists, and turned away.

Limping across the yard, he cursed between his teeth, hoping that the reverend would drive off the road and the car would burst into flames. He deserved nothing less than to burn in hell for making Emily cry.

10.

A Friend and a Foe

When Reverend Oswald had been away before, his presence could still be felt all around; in the empty seat at the table and the observation of all the rules, how plates, glasses, and cutlery were gathered after lunch, how the group walked silently out of the dining room in a single row.

But this time it was different, for after only a short and silent prayer at breakfast, Emily began chatting happily with the boys, so after a while the dining room was full of laughter and jokes, funny remarks and smiling faces. The boys finished the porridge, chatting away, while Emily sat with a broad smile on her face, beaming with joy.

Henry didn't smile, at least not on the outside, but he understood what she was doing: she was taking her own revenge on the reverend, breaking the rules while he was away. He felt for her, so much and so deeply that he wanted nothing more than to stand up and embrace her, to hold her in his arms. But he didn't move.

At lunchtime he helped Emily carry food to the boys where they were digging. They shoveled sand into sacks, stacking the sacks in a heap farther away, as if they were making a fortress.

Emily brought a large pot full of steaming goulash, their all-time favorite dish, and announced that there would be no more work today. They sat down happily in the sand and she walked among them, filling their bowls with a large ladle.

Henry limped toward where John was hacking away at the lava slab with the crowbar in his hand.

There was a small pile of stones already, which would be used later to build up the foundation, once the bedrock had been reached. John had taken off his T-shirt and was sweating; the muscles moved under his skin as he raised the crowbar and slammed it into the slab. Shards of rock shot out in all directions.

John didn't seem to notice him, so Henry cleared his throat and called out, "Lunch!"

John stopped, breathing hard, and glanced at Henry. His eyes were shining again, and Henry knew why. It was fury.

"So it's time to feed the slaves, is it?" he hissed under his breath.

Henry grinned shyly. He longed to be able to shoot back a snappy answer, something nasty about the reverend, and then he and John would laugh together like friends, and everything would be all right. But he had no idea what to say. John sighed, picked up his T-shirt, and wiped his face. He followed Henry back to where the little ones were and sat down.

Henry couldn't help but admire John's looks, his long black hair moist with sweat, his muscular body, the angry frown on his noble face. John was like a movie hero, an outlaw, wrongfully judged but determined to right all wrongs, to have his just revenge, to win back his rightful place as the true heir of his lost kingdom.

John looked up, and sparks seemed to fly from his shimmering green eyes as he searched Henry's face.

"So, are you related to them or something?" he asked.

Henry didn't give a quick answer, and John was impatient.

"The reverend and Emily?" John said.

Henry shook his head eagerly and blushed. John looked at him for a thoughtful moment, then he smiled a little.

"You don't talk much, do you?"

"No," Henry replied, searching his mind like crazy, trying to find something to say, something easy, something funny, but finding nothing.

"You don't honestly believe in it, do you?" John said with a grin. "You know: God and all that shit?"

Henry couldn't help but laugh a little, and shook his head. "I b-believe in c-cow shit," he blurted out, almost without stuttering at all. He found it so funny he could barely hold his laughter back, so he let it go. He noticed that John's face turned to stone for a second. Then he burst out laughing as well.

"This is the second time we speak," John finally said, "and we're still on the same subject: shit!" He laughed again and stood up. "It says a lot, doesn't it, about this place, I mean; that's what it is, a shithole!"

Henry laughed but tried to hold back at the same time, for it was truly too much; his stomach was aching. It wasn't what John was saying that made it so extremely funny, but the fact that John was actually speaking to him. It filled him with immense joy; John was joking with Henry, like he was really someone, like they were friends.

Emily handed them a bowl of goulash each and they started to eat.

There was a mild breeze from the south; white, puffy clouds glided across the blue sky, their shadows moving lazily up the low mountains in the north. The breeze was salty and warm and carried the spicy scent of heather and thyme from the lava all around them.

Henry wanted the moment to last forever; it was a happy moment indeed. They ate in silence, and the little boys ran off to the smithy to play or work on their huts. Emily collected the bowls into the empty pot and gave the older boys a smile.

"Take it easy now, boys," she said. "Just remember to fetch the cows on time, Henry." Then she walked to the house. John lay down in the warm sand on the knoll and stretched out his arms and legs.

"I feel like taking a nap," he said.

Henry sat still with a smile playing on his lips, looking across the lava field, watching the clouds glide overhead, unable to say anything. He was just happy. Happy.

"A shithole, that's what it is," John murmured. "Before too long I'm out of here," he went on. "Far away. Far, far away. And when that day comes, I will need your help, you know;

distracting the reverend somehow, so he doesn't notice anything until it's too late. You think you can do that?"

Henry wasn't sure what John meant; his voice had become cold and dark, a confidential whisper, and there was no joy in it any longer. But he had to nod in agreement. What John meant by "help," Henry had no idea.

"It won't happen just yet," John said in a low voice, still lying flat on his back, his gleaming green eyes shut, his noble face darkened in the shadow of a passing cloud. "Not until my friend arrives."

Henry felt something cold in his belly, like he'd swallowed an ice cube. He cleared his throat.

"Friend?" he said.

"Yeah, Mark, my best friend," John replied with a sly smile on his face. "Now there's a *real* devil for your reverend," he said, chuckling. "He can fool anyone, anywhere. He was supposed to be on the bus with me, but you know what? He ran off, just like that; the policeman looked the other way for a second, and he just disappeared, like he'd vaporized. He's a cunning one." John grinned. "I know where he went, and why. But that's a secret. When he's done what he has to do, he'll let himself be caught, and then they'll bring him here. You'll see."

Henry stood up slowly. John raised his head a little and squinted his eyes.

"I can trust you then, right?" he said.

Henry nodded. Then he turned away, limped down the knoll, and headed toward the yard. The ice he'd felt in his stomach had melted, only to reveal a huge black stone, formed like a fist, rolling about inside him with every limping step he took.

Two days later the yellow Volvo drove back into the yard. Reverend Oswald stepped out of the car along with a thin boy. He hunched his head forward but glanced quickly around the yard, as if he was expecting attack from every direction.

He wore black army boots, the shoelaces untied as if he had put them on in a hurry. He didn't have a suitcase or a bag of clothes or anything of that sort. The only thing he'd brought with him was a small harmonica in the breast pocket of his shirt.

Everything changed with the arrival of Mark. He was set to work with John in the rock mine, but Mark never wanted to do the same thing for too long. When he got bored of breaking rocks and carrying rocks and piling rocks, he just gave up and started playing his harmonica and dancing around like an idiot. They laughed a lot, John and Mark, and they were always together, hiding behind the smithy, smoking, for Mark had somehow managed to smuggle a lot of cigarettes in with him.

One day Henry was pushing the wheelbarrow toward the dung heap behind the barn, when he noticed the two of them there. He couldn't hear what they were saying, but they were laughing wickedly, lighting up their cigarettes, spitting, coughing, and grinning. They seemed to be plotting like devious mercenaries who had sneaked into the enemy's camp and were preparing to blow it all up. They didn't even notice him, or at least they didn't seem to. Henry imagined they were planning something sinister, perhaps setting the barn on fire? With the reputation they had between them, anything was possible.

Henry herded the cows eastward, thinking bitterly of the friend he'd almost had, but had lost. In the field, the ears of the longhaired grass, which moved in the soft breeze, were growing darker. Emily had mentioned that soon the Brute would come with his old tractor to mow the field. She even said that Henry might be allowed to mow the grass, as he was the oldest boy on the farm.

Thinking about that made him feel much better.

11.
The Outcast

The workdays had been scheduled so everybody knew his place in the big scheme of things. The digging group continued shoveling the sand out of the foundation hole on the knoll, west of the farmyard, and a little farther west John and Mark hewed their crowbars into the lava slab, breaking off rocks for the foundation of the church itself.

Once the digging group finally reached the bedrock below, there was a celebration with bread and jam and fruit juice. Then the digging group became the foundation builders, and began to carry the rocks from the quarry and stack them into the hole.

Two carpenters arrived from the village to oversee the work and prepare for the building of the church.

But Henry had his own duties to think of.

He woke early to fetch the cows for first milking. The mornings were still, the sky was clear, and the scent of the vegetation in the lava field filled the air. By now Henry knew every rock, every stream, and every mossy knoll along the way. It gave him comfort and a feeling of security. The cows greeted him with a friendly purr, standing by the gate in the field, relieved and glad to see him. He couldn't help the strange happy tingling reappearing in his stomach; they were his friends, the cows, his true friends. They didn't demand anything from him, but gave him everything they had to give: their gentle presence, their devotion to him, obedience. It filled him with pride that they were his herd, and his alone. They would never abandon him or betray him, never nurse an ill thought about him or find him at fault in any way. They loved him exactly as he was.

Back at the cowshed, each cow walked straight into her stall, glancing over to Noah, who mooed a masculine greeting toward them, curling his upper lip in a wide smile. The easygoing ritual of milking was the best time of the day. He tied up their tails and sat on the small stool beside each cow, washed their udders with a clean rag soaked in hot water, then put some udder grease on the teats and squeezed them, two teats at a time, in a steady rhythm, resting his forehead on the cows' bellies, listening to the pleasing sound of the milk hitting the sides of the iron bucket.

Milking felt almost like sleeping, for when he emptied the last bucket into the milk container he was completely relaxed, as if he had just woken up from a long, peaceful sleep. He filled the home container and carried it toward the house. Halfway across the yard he heard a low rumble on the road. He stopped and watched as the Brute arrived in his tractor. It was dark green with silver letters on the side. Henry's heart sped up and he hurried to take the milk inside. He returned as fast as he could to find the Brute attaching the mower to the tractor.

Henry stood beside the Brute, watching his every move as he went about his business with a wrench and a can of grease. Henry was determined to learn quickly what he needed to know, for he couldn't wait to master the art of controlling this machine, to feel the power of the engine obeying his every command.

He wanted to ask the Brute what he was doing and why, but the words were stuck in his throat. So he held his breath for a while, waiting patiently for the Brute to tell him to step up into the driver's seat, where he would show him how to go about driving it. He couldn't wait to try, couldn't wait to drive that thing, smelling the diesel fumes, listening to the roaring engine under his firm control.

But it didn't happen like that.

Reverend Oswald walked toward the tractor followed by John and Mark. The Brute gave them a short lesson and, after a little while, they rode the tractor out of the yard, following the Brute in his red pickup, the mower elevated into the air with its hundreds of sharp spikes. They took the road eastward, into the sunshine, dust dancing around the wheels to the tune of Mark's harmonica and the rumble of the diesel engine.

They had mowed half the big field by the time Henry herded the cows homeward for the evening milking. The ground was stark yellow and the fallen grass lay in dark green bundles, circle after circle on the field.

There was a strong breeze from the ocean and small white clouds galloped across the blue sky. Their shadows moved fast over the moss in the lava, gently stroking the spines of the cows before they hurried up the red pumice slopes. The wind, fresh and salty, carried with it the laughter from the field. The cows moved slowly, like a fully loaded freight train, and Henry followed, sweating from the walk, for his leg was in pain. The cows waded across the swamp in the field and the wind caught the splashing water; their hides glittered with the spray, which sprinkled him in the face. It cooled him off. He wiped his face, dried his eyes, and sniffed. His nose ran constantly in the summer warmth, but it had been a long time since he'd had this burning in his eyes. Maybe it was the salt in the wind.

The two boys were fooling around in the field, throwing fresh grass at each other, fighting, cursing, and laughing. Henry realized, with a sinking feeling that he'd been hiding from all day, that he wasn't going to get the chance to try the tractor this summer.

Maybe Reverend Oswald let John and Mark do everything because they were more miserable than he was, because they had more demons to deal with within themselves. Henry had not broken the law, gotten drunk, or stolen anything. He looked away and limped faster behind the cows, seriously regretting that he hadn't committed any decent crime.

The next morning the reverend told Henry he would have to take over in the rock mine, now that the two boys were busy mowing and harvesting. After finishing the morning milking, he had to limp toward the rock mine and slave there the whole day.

Henry felt utterly abandoned and alone, clenching his jaws as he thrust the crowbar into the rough slab, breaking off chunks of rock, one after the other.

He thought he heard the little boys whisper and giggle at him. They glanced at him with a sarcastic glint in their eyes when they came to collect the rocks and muttered as they scampered away.

All his little pleasures were ruined. Milking, herding the cows, and cleaning the dung canal became a strained effort. He had dared to hope for a friend, but instead he was an outcast.

After wrestling with Noah until he saw red, his fury finally subsided. When he rested his head against the bull's crown, Noah purred in a deep gentle tone as if he was telling him that one day everything would be all right.

But Henry doubted it.

12.
The Price of Friendship

A whole week with the crowbar in his hands and Henry was about to explode. He had produced a huge pile of rocks, so the boys had more than enough, at least for a while. Henry abandoned the rock mine and stole away to the sea cliffs, clambering down into the cave. He sat there all day long, singing with the surf, watching the birds glide on their broad wings past the mouth of the cave. He could have stayed there the whole night. When he finally got up, it wasn't because he was hungry or anything, but he saw by the sun that it was time to fetch the cows. He returned the next day, once he'd led the cows back to the field, and again the day after.

In his heart, he hoped that perhaps Emily would notice his absence and ask him what was wrong, why he broke the rules. But she didn't notice; perhaps she didn't care for him anymore. And the reverend was far too busy in his office to notice that the cowherd wasn't fulfilling his duties in the rock mine.

He had begun to wonder if the reverend was right, after all; that there really was a God and a devil constantly fighting for possession of each human soul. And perhaps some people were marked for the devil from the beginning, as the reverend had said. The devil's children, as he'd called them, are those who were conceived in lust, not love, and had to struggle and fight the demons that possessed them so their souls could be saved from the torments of hell.

And the first step to redemption was to learn the Ten Commandments.

"Remember the Ten Commandments," the reverend had said. "Learn them by heart, say them out loud in your everyday work so they become a part of your life."

Henry knew almost all the commandments from Oswald's religious lessons. He sometimes muttered the key words of every commandment to himself as he was clearing out the dung canal. Remembering the number of each one had become a fixation for him. Which was why he didn't necessarily say them in the proper order.

"Not name in vain: three. Not murder: six. Honor father-mother: five. Don't desire: ten."

Early morning and he was muttering like that, untying the cows after milking, when suddenly John was standing by his side. Henry immediately fell silent, clenching his jaw. John asked if he could help him herd the cows. Henry didn't want any help, he didn't want anyone to come with him, because when the cows were in the field he was going to his cave to sing along with the surf.

He didn't answer but sniffed for a long time. He had wiped his nose so often on the sleeve of his sweater that it was red and sore.

John followed him up to the gate, running ahead to open it and close it before and after the cows had walked through. Then John walked beside Henry while the cows found their easy rhythm on the path along the road.

Henry felt extremely uneasy having anyone so close to him, especially now, especially John. Instead of limping along in his usual slow rhythm, he became stiff and awkward and his clubfoot became difficult to manage.

"Can you keep a secret? We need your help," John said suddenly, in a hushed voice. "The reverend can't know a thing. And neither can Emily, or else all hell will break loose."

Henry cleared his nose with a horrible sound and spat. John wasn't here to help him, or to be his friend, but to find out if he could keep his mouth shut! How stupid Henry felt for imagining anything else.

Henry tightened his grip on the whip and hit his leg several times with the handle. Then he cleared his throat vigorously.

"Leave me alone," he growled. "Go away."

He limped faster to indicate that the conversation was over. But John placed his hand on Henry's shoulder and stopped him. He shouldn't have done that. Henry ripped himself free and menacingly brandished his whip, burning with rage.

"Go away!" he screeched.

He turned around, limping onward as fast as his clubfoot allowed.

But John followed.

"Henry," he called. "We need your help. We need a good place, a hiding place, somewhere in the lava, perhaps. To have a party, understand? Of course you're invited; of course you'll be with us."

Henry slowed down. His foot was aching, his nose burning.

So this was the big mystery. This was what all the whispers had been about. A party. Henry had begun to imagine that they were going to set the barn on fire, even murder Reverend Oswald.

"You must know of some good spot in the lava somewhere," John said. "Neither of us can get away long enough to find a place, you see? It needs to be somewhere we can't be heard, understand, far enough away? So we decided to ask you."

Henry sat down, out of breath, on a moss-covered rock, leaned forward, and rubbed his sore calf. The cows came to a halt and started nibbling on the grass beside the road.

John knelt by his side and explained the plan. Mark had struck a deal with the Brute, who had managed to get them some booze.

"But we need a hiding place," John said. "Then next time the reverend goes away, we'll have a wild party," he added, and grinned.

"Booze?" Henry asked.

"Of course! There's no party if there's no booze," John said, throwing his long hair backward.

Once again there was a confidential tone in his voice, just like the day when they had been laughing together. It made Henry believe for a moment that he was really important. He knew a lot of good spots in the lava field. There were enough crevasses, holes, and clefts that you could have many parties going at once and nobody would hear a thing. But he didn't want to tell John right away. It took him a long time to get rid of all the snot and slime from his nose with his fingers.

"I know a place," he finally said.

"Where?"

But Henry couldn't answer just like that. The most important thing now was not to say too much too soon, to withhold all information for as long as possible. Maybe he could hold on to this friendship a little longer if he didn't say anything right away.

"Where?" John pressed on with an air of irritation.

"First the cows," Henry replied, and stood up.

The cows began to search for their rhythm again. But now John wanted to go fast. The cows loved to walk slowly, without any sense of being rushed. Henry never hurried them, for he too liked to walk slowly, because of his leg. He was like a slow, lazy cow, walking in a gentle rhythm, in his own time.

But now John was by his side. Now he couldn't be like a cow. And there was so much to think about. It was so complicated. Henry had to pretend he didn't care about the party, had to make John feel he was doing him a huge favor.

"Can't they go any faster?" John asked, and started to urge them on with shouts and high-pitched whistles. Henry didn't like that at all. He was the one who was supposed to look after them, talk to them, and Henry knew you should never urge cows on. But he didn't say anything because he didn't want to offend John too much. The friendship was hardly anything yet. And if John started to dislike something at this point maybe there wouldn't be a friendship at all. So Henry kept his mouth shut.

John urged the cows on the way he wanted, until they were all running like mad, their udders swinging hard from side to side. Henry was afraid they might rip off.

Finally they stopped, panting and grunting by the gate, and Old Red sent him an accusing glance. She breathed fast out of her huge nostrils, with thick angry brows over her eyes. Henry pretended he didn't notice her look, but opened the gate and let them into the field. That's friendship, he thought; in order to gain it in one place you have to sacrifice it in another.

Then they started the long walk across the rugged lava. Henry tried hard to walk fast; he felt time was running out. John could lose interest if the walk took too long.

"Where is this damn place?" John sighed, obviously tired of stumbling over the lava.

Henry was out of breath and couldn't answer, but pointed and nodded eagerly. He was soaked in sweat, his leg hurt, and slime ran constantly from his nose.

Finally they arrived at the cliffs. Shipwreck Bay stretched out below them with its churning surf. A strong gust of wind blew up the high cliffs, straight into their faces, and John gasped. A white cloud of birds fell screeching out from the cliffs and stretched their wings on the wind.

"Where is this place?" John called out, and gave Henry a suspicious glance.

Maybe he was scared and thought Henry had tricked him

all this way to throw him over the edge. For a moment Henry could see the image in his mind: John turning and twisting in the air in a slow fall until the surf gobbled him up and crushed him on the rocks.

Henry sat down, swung his legs over the edge, and was about to take hold of the chain. But John jumped toward him and grabbed his arm.

"Are you crazy?" he screamed.

He hadn't noticed the chain and probably thought that Henry was going to throw himself into the abyss. Maybe he honestly thought Henry was retarded after all.

Their eyes met in a quick glance. That's friendship: it wants to save your life. Until it has gotten what it wants.

Henry raised the chain. "There's a cave," he said.

John let go of his arm. He didn't seem particularly happy. He looked rather disappointed and sat down. Henry clung to the chain, his legs dangling in the air.

"This is hopeless," John said finally. "The girls won't have the nerve to go down there."

Henry looked at the friend he had almost had, without understanding anything; what girls could he be talking about? "Girls?"

"Girls, man," John said, raising his hands with open palms to stress the importance of the word. "There's no party if there aren't any girls!"

From the look on John's face you could tell that the plan had collapsed. It was as if Henry had ruined the whole thing.

He didn't know what to do; should he cling to the chain a little longer or go home? He might just as well go down to the cave; he was going to anyway, before John came along.

Henry inched down the cliff until his feet touched the ledge. John decided to follow.

They entered the cave and John looked around. His face lit up.

"Great place," he said. "Damn great place!" he added, taking a cigarette out of his pocket and lighting it. Now John was happy. He had a smoke and smiled.

He didn't offer Henry a cigarette. Of course Henry wouldn't have accepted it, because he hated the smell of cigarettes, but nevertheless it would have been a gesture of friendship. Henry thought it would also have been polite if John had asked Henry first if he minded smoking in here.

But John didn't ask. And the awful smell filled up the cave as John went on about the party and the girls they were inviting, the girls he and Mark had met on the road while mowing the fields. The smoke stung Henry's eyes and the foul smell made him sick. Suddenly he felt unwelcome in his own private sanctuary, which he'd foolishly given away in the hope of gaining John's friendship. But now Henry realized it hadn't turned out the way he'd hoped.

Maybe John hadn't meant anything by inviting Henry to the party; maybe Henry had misunderstood. What was *he* supposed to do at a party with girls, anyway? They'd be scared of him or laugh at him. He should have kept his mouth shut. Now the cave was no longer his place to come and sing with the surf. All things considered, it would have been far better to continue being the idiot in the cowshed who knew nothing. Besides, this party thing was bound to be against all the rules—and the commandments. Henry had traded his precious secret for the friendship he desired. But he'd gained nothing from it.

Don't desire: ten, he thought. But it was too late to change that now.

13.

The Devil's Children

And the rain arrived.

Gray drapes glided across the ocean, dragging their hem over the land. The mountains in the north were covered in a white mist that wove around the ridge, stretching out over the lava fields and blocking every view. Only the nearest surroundings were visible, a stretch of lava and the white farmhouses with their red roofs. It rained from every angle. The wind pounded Henry's face with water as he came around the corner. His feet splashed with every step, and the cows' cloven hooves sank deep into the mud by the gate.

John and Mark had finally finished mowing the field. The tractor stood by the barn wall with the mower raised. The sharp edges of the blades were coated in bits of grass. In weather like this there was nothing to do but wait; wait for the rain to stop, wait, wait. No work could be done on the foundations of the church either, for the sand ran everywhere. Nor was there any point in breaking the lava slabs into rocks in this kind of weather. It was out of the question. But not for Henry.

After milking, he limped across the yard without a dry thread on his clothes. He found the crowbar and dragged it behind him, toward the quarry. Grabbing it with both hands, he struck the lava with all his might. His rage gave him power, like a force of nature, like a giant crunching the earth beneath his feet. The rain poured down and the storm pelted water against his face and shoulders, but he hardly noticed it. It felt good to break rocks in the howling wind and the hissing rain, felt good to squeeze the cold iron crowbar, to raise it high and then strike it against the lava, which cracked with a hollow sigh.

It felt good to work like crazy when he didn't have to. He wasn't working for the reverend. He wasn't working for anyone. He was doing it because he was furious.

He raised the crowbar high and thrust it down with all his might. A piece of rock broke off the lava, and the raindrops drilled the earth, hammering his forehead like nails.

He had given his cave to John and nothing had changed. John didn't come to talk to him. It was just as he'd known it would be; they would never be friends.

He didn't want John's friendship, anyway. He just wanted to be left alone.

Suddenly he was exhausted and threw the crowbar to the ground and stormed back to his room. He stood for a long time in the quiet until his head was finally empty of curses.

The tempest subsided during the night.

In the morning, Henry heard the yellow Volvo honk farewell at the gate as Oswald drove to the city. The car disappeared down the road. This was the chance John and Mark had been waiting for; Henry knew the party would be tonight.

Right after breakfast John and Mark attached the large metal tedder, which would rake the hay, to the tractor and drove to the field. The spikes glowed in the bright sun; the air was thick and warm.

It was a laundry day and Emily had hung linens on the clothesline behind the farmhouse. The fresh breeze filled the white sheets and duvet covers like sails on a large ship that cut the waves on the black lava ocean.

When he'd herded the cows to pasture after morning milking, Henry went straight to the rock mine. He stacked the rocks he'd been mining the day before, but he didn't have the energy to do much else, so he just sat there, dozing off in the sun.

Emily brought sandwiches for lunch. The little ones crowded around her, happily enjoying her company, but Henry sat aside. He wondered if he should tell her about the party, but then decided to say nothing. After all, he'd provided the cave, so in a way he was an accessory to the crime-not-yet-committed. He felt guilty and looked away when Emily glanced at him, smiling.

It was close to evening by the time John and Mark drove back to the farm. Henry was leading the cows to pasture after evening milking when the green tractor suddenly appeared on the dusty road. John sat at the wheel, bare to the waist, and Mark sat on the fender beside him. The rake was suspended high in the air behind them, the wheels rotating slowly, the pikes shimmering. This was their victory chariot. They were like soldiers coming home from war, full of pride for their deeds on the battlefield, young and excited, with a great feast awaiting them. They didn't notice him, or pretended not to. The cows became afraid of the racket caused by the diesel engine and kicked their hooves, pricked up their ears, and flared their nostrils, while the monstrous rear wheels gobbled up the dusty road.

John and Mark talked loudly to each other and laughed like grown men. Mark was wearing a red T-shirt with a light jacket tied around his waist. He raised a tight fist and shouted, making the veins bulge on his forehead and his neck. John joined in. They were heroes.

Henry stood in the swamp, below the road. He couldn't go any farther because the cows wouldn't move until the danger had passed. As they came closer, Mark ripped off his T-shirt and swung it like a battle flag above his head, shaking his fist at Henry with his other hand, and bellowed a war cry. John lifted one hand from the steering wheel, as if greeting Henry, and held it still in the air while the victory chariot rumbled by in a cloud of brown dust and the stench of diesel fumes.

The wheels on the rake squeaked as the faded pikes slowly turned another circle.

Henry had a hard time falling asleep that night. He was kind of hoping that John would come and invite him to join them in the cave. After all, it was his cave. But John didn't mean anything he'd said. He didn't care about Henry. They could go to hell anyway. Henry thought about when John raised his hand off the steering wheel. He'd probably been mocking him. Maybe the gesture was his way of saying, "Here I am, riding my warhorse, and there you are, stuck in a bog behind your cows' asses." He should wake Emily up and expose them. Then they would get their punishment on Reverend Oswald's return.

But then he was also hoping that John wouldn't invite him at all. His mother had sometimes had parties when he was small. She'd drink with ugly men who bellowed loudly while she lay limp and silent, the apartment engulfed in a gray cloud of cigarette smoke, bottles falling over on the coffee table. Then, sometimes, he had gotten scared.

No. He was not interested in parties.

He tossed and turned under the duvet and tried to sleep, but his heartbeat kept him awake. The longer he lay, squeezing his eyes shut, the more relieved he felt that John hadn't invited him to join them. But, at the same time, he wondered if John had ever intended to anyway. Then he became angry. Vacillating between relief and anger, he tried to fall asleep.

But just as sleep was finally gaining the upper hand, he heard the cowshed door open. A second later someone peeped into his room, chuckling in the dark.

A foul stench of booze filled the room, as Mark stepped in and sat on his clothes, which lay on the chair. Mark was holding a bottle, which was lit up by the dim moonlight coming through the window. He was smoking.

"Listen," he said, inhaling sharply and then exhaling. "There's a problem. We just have two girls. But there are three of us. Three boys, two girls: trouble. Cute girls even. Phew. A big problem.

"John asked me to tell you," he went on, "that maybe it would be better if you joined us next time. What do you say about that? This won't be our last party, and that's a promise."

Henry lay rigidly in his bed with the duvet covering him. For some reason he was suddenly afraid of Mark, and the familiar troll's fist punched his stomach from inside. The boy seemed somehow bigger and more threatening, all smiling and happy with a little booze in his head.

"This is for you," Mark said, handing him the bottle.

Henry had never tasted alcohol. He had seen how it changed normal people into monsters. He was enough of a monster as it was. And it smelled awful as well.

"G-go away," he said.

Mark put the bottle on the floor and stood up with the cigarette dangling from the corner of his mouth.

"Unfortunately the mixers are all in the cave," he said. "But I've always liked it best unmixed; straight from the cow, as they say," he added with a grin.

Then he staggered out and closed the door behind him.

Henry was relieved for only a moment, and then full of fury. Why did John have to send Mark? Why hadn't he come himself? And why did he send a bottle? What was Henry supposed to do with it, drink it on his own?

He turned to face the wall, rolled the duvet between his legs, determined to sleep. But he could feel his heart beating fast in his ear, which was pressed against the pillow. He turned onto his other side.

On the floor stood the bottle from John.

What an idiot Henry had been, imagining a friendship just because John had asked him about the east and north, just because they'd laughed together on the knoll that day. What a fool he had been when John had pretended to be helping him with the cows. How stupid to let Mark go so easily. He should have beaten him up, taken the bottle and smashed it in his grinning face. What an idiot.

He pulled the duvet off and sat up with a thousand screaming seagulls in his head. Before he knew it he was fully dressed, walking down Spine Break Path with the bottle in his hand, as fast as his clubfoot would allow him. He was going to give the bottle back to John and tell him to rot in hell.

There was a half-moon in the purple night sky. The breeze from the cliffs brought with it echoes of girly screeches. Henry lay on the edge and looked down. A small fire was burning on the ledge outside his cave. He heard the voices of John and Mark telling the girls tall tales about themselves. They talked fast and loud, interrupting each other all the time. The girls gasped and whined with laughter.

"Thank you, my sordid Lord," Mark said in a sanctimonious voice, imitating Emily saying grace at dinner. "Thank you for the grub and the fat and the shit that I shat. Amen and hallelujah!"

The laughter seemed to come from every direction, even the ocean. The surf giggled; the cliffs chuckled. And there was music too, a demonic sound that made the rocks tremble.

"Cheers!" John shouted. Then bottles clinked.

Henry stretched his neck farther over the edge, turning his head a little, pricking up his ears. One girl appeared at the mouth of the cave and asked if there was somewhere she could pee. Mark said she could just place her bottom over the ledge and let go. "The biggest toilet in the world!" he said, laughing.

There was a rattling from the chain, then three dark figures crawled up the steep path. Henry jumped to his feet and limped for cover in a hollow close by.

Three girls climbed with ease up to the ledge, three elves from the underworld, looking around them for a good place to pee. John's worries had obviously been unfounded, because they didn't seem to be afraid of heights in the least. Three girls, black around the eyes, with purple nail polish and flaming red lips. One in a very wide T-shirt and miniskirt with a dog-collar necklace around her neck. Another with a teddy-bear backpack hanging over her shoulder. The third pointed with a glowing cigarette across the lava field, and the three of them tiptoed over the sharp rocks.

Three girls. One each if Henry had been invited. Somehow this lie was the worst of all.

They squatted in a circle, facing one another like witches, peeing in the lava and throwing glowing cigarette stubs in all directions, whispering about who should get which boy.

One liked John, another liked Mark, but one was afraid of Mark, and the one who liked John agreed Mark was disgusting. They put on more lipstick and ruffled their hair, squawking like seagulls in coarse voices as they inched themselves back down the chain. The demonic music grew louder as soon as they disappeared over the edge.

Henry stayed still, taking in what they'd said. If Mark was disgusting, what was Henry? He wasn't even good enough to be invited, even though there were too many girls. He was a monster. No doubt about it anymore. Henry lay still and looked at the moon. It looked like half a face, peeping from behind a dark curtain. Maybe God's spy, checking what the naughty children were doing while the good children were sleeping.

"The devil's children," as Reverend Oswald had called them. "Intoxication and Lust are their parents," he had said. "They will have to live with that dreadful legacy, unless they accept Jesus Christ as the master of their lives. Only then can the devil's children receive forgiveness," he'd said.

The Peeping Tom in the sky looked down upon Henry with a furrowed brow. He was also a devil's child, begotten in the multiple sins of his mother, who probably didn't even know who his father was. Why does God allow the devil's children to be born? Henry wondered. Is it so that they can be saved? And what of those who don't get saved? Are they outcasts forever?

It was easy to understand why the devil was lonely and wanted to make friends. Jesus was, of course, very good and all that, and that's why he had so many friends. That wasn't a problem when your dad happened to be God Almighty, who lived in heaven where everybody wants to be. The devil has nothing except himself and his loneliness. Why shouldn't he try to win people over by every conceivable means? The devil's children were his children, so why couldn't he have them in peace?

The eye of the moon moved slowly above the moss-covered lava and the music boomed out over the silver ocean. The surf rumbled in a deep voice, churning sleepily down below, in the bewitching lap of the waves.

Henry wasn't sure if he fell asleep.

When he opened his eyes the music had stopped, the moon had disappeared, and the sky was gray. White wisps of fog glided over the lava like ghosts. He stumbled to his feet and looked around him. The bottle from John lay on the ground. Now he wished he'd had the nerve to tell Emily everything the day before, for he suspected that if she learned of this later, John and Mark would say that he had been involved. Perhaps she wouldn't believe them, but the reverend would. Oh, yes, the reverend would punish Henry too, just in case, as a warning.

He owed nothing to the two friends who now slept peacefully in the cave, but he owed it to himself to speak up, before it was too late.

For hadn't the Lord said: The truth will set you free?

14.

The Cairn of Christ

Reverend Oswald climbed the cairn in his shiny shoes, took the top stone with the white cross, and climbed down again.

"The first shall be last," he said in a somber tone of voice.

He drew a big circle beside the cairn with the heel of his shiny shoe. Then he turned to Henry.

"You will not be going to sleep tonight," he said, "for tonight you will rebuild this cairn inside this circle here, stone by stone, before the sun rises tomorrow morning."

Henry bowed his head.

"You might not see the point," Reverend Oswald continued, "but therein lies your lesson. Since you broke the rules, by not telling us what you knew, but instead deciding to assist John and Mark in their wicked ways, you will work one night for no purpose, in the name of Jesus Christ. Remember this, Henry: this is not a punishment; this is a project from which I hope you will learn a hard lesson. May God be with you." Then he walked across the yard and disappeared into the house.

Henry stood for a while, looking up at the cairn, wondering what would have happened if he'd kept silent. He had taken the bottle to Emily and told her everything. But she already knew, for the police in the village had contacted her: three girls from the village had come home in the early hours. When their parents asked what happened, they started to cry and said that two boys from the home had forced them to drink, and they had made other, darker, accusations.

Henry was certain he would never forget the look on Emily's face when she realized that he was an accomplice to the crime.

"You knew? And you only tell me now?" she'd asked, hoping she had misunderstood. But she hadn't. And Henry knew he had broken her heart.

˙He hadn't said a word until he'd realized that there was a possibility that he could have been blamed also. If only he had kept his mouth shut he wouldn't be here now.

He climbed the cairn and grabbed the first stone, took it in his arms, crawled backward, and placed it in the middle of the circle that the reverend had made on the ground.

The stones were equal in size, each one almost the breadth of his chest, and they stacked nicely. But they were cut from lava rock and had a rough surface, which tore at Henry's skin. And the stones were heavy.

When he had moved five stones he felt it would take him days to finish. Twenty stones later the palms of his hands were scratched and bleeding. Forty stones, and the lack of purpose was screaming in his face. He just wanted to go to bed and fall asleep.

Besides, he had no idea if he was doing this right or if the whole thing was going to collapse over his head.

Mark had been locked in the Boiler Room, John in a room in the attic. That was their punishment, praying on their knees with Reverend Oswald. It could have been worse, for the village police had come to interrogate them, but the reverend said he would punish them sufficiently here. Then a government official arrived and questioned the two boys. Then he'd talked to the little ones. He heard about them slaving away on the foundations of the church, and further investigations were called for. Then a decision was quickly made: this was no home for little children; they would be taken away. It was a shock to the reverend. Henry had been in the kitchen and heard him argue with the official.

"A breach of faith," the official called it. "We trust you to give these children a good education and a healthy life on your farm; not to use them for manual labor." The official looked stern. "We'll send for them when we've found them a new place to stay. Consider yourself lucky that we aren't closing this place down permanently. The older boys can stay, but it is clear to us that you are not equipped to care for young children."

It was getting dark.

The faint sound of the distant waves by the cliffs grew louder in the stillness, like the surf was coming closer in the darkness, threatening to engulf him. A chilly shudder went through Henry. He climbed the cairn and worked like mad, carrying rocks from one pile to the other. As night fell, the wind picked up and a cool breeze whispered in his ears. As soon as he stopped to catch his breath the sweat cooled on his body and he shivered, so he kept on going. The cairn didn't seem to grow any smaller where it stood and didn't seem to get any larger where it was supposed to stand. His back and arms ached, his fingers were swollen and bleeding, he was tired and sleepy, all alone in the pale night.

He clearly heard the sounds of the night from the lava field. Maybe they were birds or some other animals, foxes or minks. Didn't animals sleep at night? He thought he heard a faint sound from invisible wings above his head. He stopped moving and listened, pressed the rock to his chest and felt his heart pounding against it.

A cold shudder shot through him as he peered into the dusk. He thought he saw something pale moving over the lava field. Then he heard someone sigh, or were they sobbing? Perhaps it was a ghost, one of the small children who had been carried out here to die in past ages.

He remembered when he'd walked past the Gallows once and had almost fallen into the deepest crevasse he'd ever come across in the whole lava field. It seemed like a bottomless pit, full of darkness. He'd lain on the edge, looking down for a long time, until he'd noticed bones near the bottom; white bones, delicate and tiny. And he remembered a bird chirping in the distance and pearl drops of water on the green moss, the fragile bones moist with dew in the black crevasse.

The sun was already up when he put the last stone in place, the top stone with the white cross. There was a gray hue on the mountains and a cool breeze. Autumn was drawing near, he could feel it. Very soon he would be fetching the cows from pasture for the last time this summer. The ocean was darker than usual and the noise of the surf deeper.

His fingers were bleeding, but he didn't feel the pain. He didn't feel sleepy either, or hungry. It was still too early for breakfast, he knew; still too early to fetch the cows. So he limped down Spine Break Path toward Shipwreck Bay, climbed down the chain, and crawled into the cave. There were empty bottles there, plastic bags, and the floor was littered with cigarette butts. He threw everything over the edge until the cave was clean.

Then he sat for a long time surrounded by the droning of the surf.

If the fallen archangel could hope for forgiveness, couldn't he allow himself to hope as well? They were both equally despised and outcast. The hurt in Emily's eyes pierced through him like a knife; losing her trust was the worst thing that could have happened. He had no one but himself to blame for that. And now he had no one else to turn to but God.

He pulled his clubfoot under himself, knelt, and clasped his hands.

"Dear God," he whispered.

Then he didn't know what more to say. Maybe he should ask God to make Emily understand that he wasn't really guilty of anything, that whatever she blamed him for, he hadn't done it on purpose. But God would easily see through such a selfish wish, for God knew his thoughts exactly.

He remembered that Reverend Oswald had once said that the devil was selfish and proud, miserable, scared, and lonely because the world hated him. Perhaps if he prayed as well for the fallen archangel, then God would understand that his intentions weren't selfish but honest; he had only wanted a friend, just as the archangel did, who suffered alone in the shadow of the world.

He wasn't sure he was choosing the right words but hoped that God, who understood everything, would also understand his mumbling and take his intentions into account. He rested his head on his clasped hands and drew a deep breath.

"Dear God," he said. "Forgive us. We are very sorry for everything. We didn't mean to be bad. We just want a friend. Amen."

He muttered these words in a low voice with long silent intervals while the surf frothed and foamed down below and the rumbling shook the cliff wall. He said them out loud into the noise and released the birds that had been flying around in his mind for so long.

15.

A Summer's End

On a bright morning the two carpenters appeared and began to raise the beams for the walls of the church. Some days they came in the afternoon, sat on the foundation, had their coffee, looked over the lava field, and went away without doing anything. On other days they came right after lunch and worked like crazy till evening.

And little by little the skeleton began to take form. Beams were bolted to the foundations, corner poles rose, then vertical beams between those and more beams until the shape of windows could be seen, three on each side. Once that phase had been completed, the carpenters didn't show up for days, because a gale from the southwest brought heavy rain. When it had blown over, they appeared again with another two men and began to raise the roof beams.

The little ones stood in a group in the yard, looking west across the lava, where the symbol of victory was taking shape. Some of them walked over to watch the carpenters at work, but were told to get lost and go home. So the boys had to content themselves with watching from a distance as the church rose steadily from the ground. They could picture the layers of rocks below, far into the ground, right down to the flat rock underneath. The hole had been deep and they had filled it up, stone by stone, layer after layer, until the foundation stood well above the ground. But what did it matter? They would be gone in a week, anyway. And Henry doubted any of them would ever take that Sunday ride with their own children, as Reverend Oswald had once proudly predicted, to show them where they had slaved away in their youth for God and the reverend.

Henry watched the small group of boys out of the corner of his eye, wondering if this would indeed be a summer that they'd never forget, as the reverend had promised, or a summer they'd try hard never to remember.

On a quiet morning, with neither wind nor rain, shots from the nail gun rang out over the lava field. The carpenters fastened plywood to the skeleton, nailed boards on the roof, fitted arched frames for the windows, put tar paper on the roof, and made a rough, makeshift door. Then for another three days the iron-saw wailed as they cut the corrugated iron, and the hammers rang on the metal as they nailed it to the walls and roof. Then they were gone, and so too was the money in the church fund.

John and Mark were free from their imprisonment and were put to work, painting the panels inside the church. At breakfast, John's eyes were dull, his face worn, like that of an old man. Mark's mocking grin had disappeared, but his eyes were on fire and shot sparks in Henry's direction. The reverend looked tired as well, his beard no longer neatly groomed, his hands looking thinner when he clasped them in prayer. And the prayers weren't said out loud, but in silence.

Emily didn't join them at meals, but ate alone in the kitchen. Henry knew she and the reverend had been arguing; he'd heard their angry voices when he'd brought the milk to the house. He felt sorry for her. She was going to miss the little ones, and he knew she blamed the reverend, that much Henry had heard and understood. But Henry blamed himself too. After all, he'd disappointed her as well.

"You ask me to be a mother to all these boys," Henry had heard her say. "Yet you deny me a child of my own."

"Jesus Christ himself is our child," the reverend had replied in an angry tone. "Every boy who God sends us is in fact Jesus himself. How can there be a mightier and more worthy mission?"

Emily had begun to cry, her voice fading into a whisper. "And now they're being taken away from us. And it's all your fault."

Then the day came when Henry fetched the cows for the last time that autumn. One everlasting summer behind him and an everlasting winter approaching. He wondered if the cows realized they wouldn't be herded to the field the next morning. There was a touch of regret in their heavy breathing and moaning as they waddled across the swamp. They hung their heads while he opened the gate, and Old Red, who always walked through the gate first, stood still and let the others go in first and was the last to follow. She knew. They walked in silence down the driveway with regretful movements. Henry shared their feelings; his best moments were on the slow walk with the cows, whether the sun was shining or the rain was pouring. It wasn't until they came to the cowshed that they began to tussle and scream. And when each and every one was in her stall they lay down heaving heavy sighs, in total surrender to the injustice and indifference of this cruel world.

Noah was sure to be happier though, now that his wives were back for good. Henry thought guiltily that he had neglected his friend since John's arrival. But Noah curled his upper lip eagerly, pushed against the fence around his stall, scratched the floor, and rolled his eyes. These were certain signs of joy.

As Henry hung his whip on the nail above the door he noticed the red pickup truck drive into the yard. It was the Brute with a team of four strong men.

Reverend Oswald came out of the house and spoke to them for a minute. One of the men started the tractor and drove it toward the sheep dens. Then he lowered the tractor gallows until they touched the ground. Another one took a thick hank of rope from the pickup and carried it on his shoulder, while the third man was holding something wrapped in brown cloth. They waited by the pickup until Reverend Oswald went back inside. Then they followed the Brute toward the cowshed.

Emily stood by the garage and herded the little ones inside. Mark paced around the yard, following the men with his eyes. John sat outside the smithy.

The men crowded into the doorway of the cowshed and walked straight toward Noah's stall, muzzled him, and opened the stall. Two men held the muzzle tightly, each on one side, but the Brute shoved his fingers into the bull's nostrils and squeezed so hard Noah bellowed from pain. When the Brute pulled, Noah was forced to follow. That's how they got him out into the yard. The men then fastened ropes to the muzzle on each side. They tied one rope securely to the tractor's gallows while the four of them held the other rope firmly.

Noah stood in the yard in front of the sheep den, out in the fresh air for the first time in ages, muzzled to a tractor and tugged by four men.

He snorted and blinked his eyes toward the setting sun. Then he began to fight the ropes, kick the gravel, and roll his long tongue around the tight muzzle. His mouth foamed as he tried to gnaw the rope that dug into the corners of his mouth.

The men were quick and able with their sleeves rolled up their muscular arms, tugging at the rope with their strong hands and holding him at bay. The bull jerked his head and swung his tail angrily so it hit his flank with a loud crack. Saliva dripped from his gaping mouth and thick muscles moved under the black hide.

It was fine weather, the sky partly clouded and not really cold. But the clouds were moving fast so that now and again a beam of golden sunlight ran across the yard, gleaming in the bull's eyes.

From the garage, a droning organ could be heard.

The bull lowered his head and tried to run. The men

were dragged with him but dug their heels in the gravel and managed to pull him back. The Brute unwrapped the cloth from around a rifle and a long knife, which he placed on the ground. He pulled a bullet from his pocket and loaded the weapon. Then he walked in front of the bull, talking in a soothing voice, as if to calm him down, holding the rifle down by his leg so the beast wouldn't notice it. Noah turned his ears and eyes to the man, his nostrils flared with heavy breathing. The Brute slowly raised the rifle, pressing the barrel of the gun against Noah's curly black forehead, right between his eyes. They looked each other in the eye for just a second.

The stretched rope creaked a little when the shot rang out. The blast echoed between the buildings, the smoke coiling around the black head as the beast raised itself with a sudden jerk up on its hind legs.

Then everything went still.

But Noah didn't fall. He stood, immovable as a rock, staring at his executioner, spreading his nostrils and bellowing. The Brute lowered the weapon, unable to believe his own eyes. The devil just stood there with a bullet in his head, scratching the gravel, pulling at the ropes. The bullet must have got stuck in his thick skull. To add insult to injury, Noah rolled his upper lip and sprayed slime out of his nostrils as he laughed out loud at the wimp holding his rifle with trembling hands. The men shouted and told the Brute to hurry up. He fumbled in his pockets for another bullet, but the beast fought the ropes so they creaked and cracked, and the men had to use all their strength to hold him back.

The Brute loaded the second bullet into the rifle, raised it quickly up to his cheek, and fired a second time. The smoke curled around the outstretched ears and Noah's head jerked backward. His neck bones creaked as his head swung to one side and his front legs rose in the air.

Then he collapsed with all his weight onto the gravel, and the ground trembled.

The long machete lay on the gravel, sharpened many times, the edge gleaming. The executioner threw the rifle away, grabbed the long knife, and knelt by Noah's head. Placing the shiny edge at the throat, he sank the glistening blade into the black hide, right up to the spine. Blood gushed out of the gaping wound, as he pushed the blade with all his strength, loosening the head from the body with a firm movement and throwing it to one side. The monstrous body twitched on the ground for a while; the cloven hooves kicked the gravel sideways as if they were trying to run away. A powerful stream gushed from the open neck in a steady beat, and a wailing sound squeezed out of the throat, a long drawn cry that finally faded. The body trembled in horrific spasms and the tail hit the flank for the last time.

The sun appeared and disappeared behind a cloud. The beams ran across the yard and golden spots glimmered in the blood that floated over the gravel.

"A tough devil," one of the men said, lighting a cigarette. Another one began to cut holes through the hind legs of the bull so that they could hoist him up on the tractor and take him away to skin and butcher him. The Brute rubbed his cheeks and said he'd never experienced anything like it.

Henry stood over his friend's head and watched the blood escape.

He felt dizzy.

The singing of the little ones could be heard coming from somewhere, accompanied by Emily's loud organ. She'd probably ushered them into the garage so they wouldn't have to witness the scene. They must have been singing the whole time; he just hadn't noticed until now.

If you're happy and you know it clap your hands.
If you're happy and you know it clap your hands.
If you're happy and you know it and you really want to show it,
if you're happy and you know it clap your hands.

The men stood in a group like in an old photograph, wearing dirty jeans with their shirts hanging over their belts, cigarettes between their fingers, or arms crossed over their broad chests, watching him. The dust hung in the air, and a single beam of sunlight ran across the yard, sparkling on the black hide.

If you're happy and you know it stomp your feet.
If you're happy and you know it stomp your feet.
If you're happy and you know it and you really want to show it,
if you're happy and you know it stomp your feet.

Henry looked at his friend's head and suddenly realized that God didn't rule the world at all; neither did the devil. It was people. It wasn't really the Brute who had murdered Noah; he was just an obedient servant. It was the reverend who had done it to make more money.

Henry clenched his fists and growled deep down in his throat. He looked up and stared at the reverend's servant, the poor wretch who had performed the evil deed for his master. Never before had he looked any man so straight in the face. The other men began to move a little as they saw Henry approach.

Before the Brute knew what was happening, a heavy fist crashed into his nose and he fell to the ground. The boy threw himself on top of him and punched his face, in a steady rhythm, with the two powerful hands that had once wrestled a bull in the name of friendship. Now these same hands viciously avenged the murder of his only friend.

When the men screamed and tried to drag him away, he brushed them off like flies and continued pounding the creature that had crushed his heart on this calm autumn day. Then there was a sharp pain on the back of his head and the world went black.

16.

A Journey in the Dark

He was lost in thick darkness, and there was a terrible pain in the back of his head. He tried to move but he was paralyzed, tried to scream but no sound came out. Something had happened, he knew, something horrible, but he couldn't remember what. He had to find out, it was important, he had to know. But he was in darkness and he couldn't move; he could barely breathe. Maybe he was dead.

Then came the voice, a very soft voice, calm and reassuring. He had to listen to the voice, it was saying something important, something about friends, about missing someone you love, about seeing what is important. And there was something about a prince and a fox. It was a story.

Then everything went black again.

Some time later he opened his eyes and didn't recognize the room. He was alone. There was an old-fashioned cabinet by the wall with a large mirror on one of the doors. Some clothes were laid out on a chair, but they weren't his. The wallpaper was cream colored with tiny red flowers that at first looked like specks of blood. But there was a distinctive scent in the room that he recognized, coming from the open cabinet, a spicy scent full of warmth and sunshine. He was certain he knew that scent, but from where he failed to remember.

His head was a mountain; his eyes lay under the mountain and he couldn't move them. Was he frozen or had he melted? His hands and feet were fence posts, sinking slowly into the swamp. His mouth was dry, his tongue a kelp-covered rock, half buried in the black sand. Each moment was an eternity; time stood still, but the same instant perpetually repeated itself.

How many days and nights? He couldn't tell. He didn't care. Then blackness engulfed him again and he was lost and utterly alone and terribly afraid.

He woke up with a sore throat and hot eyes. Had he been weeping? Had someone maybe heard him? He lay still with his eyes closed and a feeling of shame. Then he felt the touch of a warm towel on his forehead. He opened his eyes and saw Emily sitting by his bedside. He suddenly felt a powerful urge to rise up and hug her, snuggle up to her tightly and continue to weep forever. The longing was so overwhelming he had to double up and face the wall.

Then he realized he was lying in her bedroom in the farmhouse.

She asked him if he was hungry, if he'd like some hot soup. He just folded his arms around his head. He didn't really want anything, just to hug her tightly. And when she was gone he noticed for the first time that he was wearing pajamas he'd never seen before. They were white with red stripes, and gave off a pleasant scent of soap and salty breeze from hanging on the clothesline.

She'd washed him and put him to bed like an infant while he was unconscious. She was definitely the best person in the world. It was like he had died and gone to hell but then woken up in heaven, wearing perfumed pajamas.

The only sound he heard outside was the quick chirping from the tiny gray bird with the long black tail.

When he sat up he felt dizzy. He rested his head in his hands for a moment, looking at the floor. Then he remembered that he hadn't seen his only friend in the world for days, maybe weeks. He had no idea how long.

He stood up slowly and leaned on the wall on his way down the stairs and went out of the door.

The sun was burning white, so he covered his eyes.

He stumbled, barefoot, in his new pajamas, across the yard. Behind him he heard Emily calling his name.

The cowshed was dark and gloomy, the floor cool under his feet.

Who was taking care of the cows now? Someone had to fetch them and milk them. He should get dressed and get going.

The fence around Noah's stall was open. Noah wasn't there. The stall was empty. And now he remembered the song, the happy song, the clap your hands song. He stood in Noah's stall, breathing in the emptiness around him. Then he screamed. Yelling out the wordless grief as the memory of his friend's last moments on Earth came back to him.

Emily came rushing through the door, and he fell to his knees.

Then he sank into the gentle embrace of utter darkness.

His consciousness stirred as he felt a spoon with warm soup on his lips. Then a glass of cold water. Then his head fell back on the soft pillow and his mind kept on falling, further downward, deeper into the abyss where there was neither light nor sound.

His eyes opened and he was standing in the bathroom. Someone was holding him up on his feet while he took a pee. Out of the corner of his eye he saw Emily reflected in the mirror, standing behind him, making sure he didn't fall over. He saw his own pale face, like a dead man's, his eyes bloodshot. She helped him back to bed, where he died once more. His heavy body sank into the soft white grave of fresh linen as his spirit flew away, out of the window, ascending ever higher into the sky.

Darkness came once more and he was lost, deep in a strange forest somewhere. But there was a voice, a tiny voice whispering to him. Perhaps the Lord had sent him an angel after all.

In the dark, pictures began to emerge, in shafts of light, like when sunbeams find their way through the thick foliage of a forest roof. It was an enchanted forest with talking rabbits and scheming wolves, with clever little boys and girls who managed to trick the witch and eat her house, to ensnare the wolf and cook it in a pot. What joy! And then there were princes and princesses, singing dwarfs, an evil stepmother talking to a mirror, a brave knight, and a duckling who froze in a pond but then turned into a swan. How beautiful!

The darkness came alive with wonders he had never known,

never heard of before. And far away in the background of it all he could just barely hear the thin voice whispering to him, painting those pictures with words, making way for the light pouring into the darkness.

Little by little his heart found its way through the enchanted forest, and his mind was finally at rest behind his eyelids.

When he opened his eyes he saw a boy sitting by the bed with a book in his lap, reading out loud. A tiny boy, thin and fragile, with curly blond hair glowing in the sunlight that seeped through the window. His small mouth twitched with every word he read, as if he was tasting the words before he read them out loud. Henry watched him for a while and wondered if he was ever going to stop. Finally Henry cleared his throat. The boy suddenly stopped, but didn't raise his head at first. Only his eyes moved slowly up from the page, over the brim of the book until they met Henry's. His eyes were large and blue. When he realized Henry was awake he jumped to his feet. The book fell to the floor, and the boy ran out.

Henry was relieved to see that he was back in his own room.

On the chair were clean clothes, neatly folded, and on the floor his specially made shoes, polished and shiny. He felt as if he had finally arrived home after a long, hard journey; he felt rested now and terribly hungry.

The cows greeted him with their moos as he entered the cowshed. He scratched Old Red behind the ears and patted her on the belly. Her eyes were full of warmth and tenderness. He noticed that the stalls and the dung canal were clean. Some-one had obviously taken care of everything while he lay in bed. But when he limped past the small window by the door he stopped in his tracks. The windowsill in the cowshed was full of books. Shiny picture books and illustrated fairy tales stood side by side in a proud row, almost filling up the window. Henry couldn't help but snort angrily. He spat on the floor and stumbled out the door.

The yellow Volvo wasn't in the yard, so Henry knew that the reverend was away. When he entered the kitchen the small boy was sitting on the chair beside the stove. And Emily was frying rye pancakes. She was laughing at something the boy had said. Then she glanced over her shoulder and smiled.

"Henry, dear. Come in, sit down."

But Henry didn't sit down, because the boy was in his favorite seat, the chair by the stove. He could have taken another chair, but he didn't. Suddenly he was filled with a strange regret, as if he didn't belong there anymore, as if the little boy had arrived to take his place.

Emily came toward him and hugged him.

"I'm so glad that you're up and feeling better," she said. "I was quite worried about you. But the doctor assured us that you'd be fine."

She continued to talk, but Henry barely heard what she said; something about someone who had hit him on the head so he'd fallen unconscious on the ground. Something about high fever and that he'd been in bed for a very long time. It felt like a lifetime.

"And here's Ollie," she said, and turned to the little boy. "He comes from the North, and will be staying with us. He's a little bookworm," she said, and ruffled the boy's hair. He giggled shyly.

"He's been sitting by your bedside every day, reading for you," she added with a smile.

The boy smiled nervously. Henry noticed he had freckles on his nose and a crooked front tooth. Emily buttered a warm rye pancake and put it on a plate.

"He's also been helping me out in the cowshed while you were ill," she said.

That information didn't make Henry feel any better. It was obvious that Emily was fond of the little boy. And why shouldn't she be? He was sweet and pretty, with big blue eyes. Not ugly and crippled. And he was a bookworm as well.

"Find a chair, Henry, and have some pancakes with us," she said.

But Henry didn't want to sit down. He looked at the pancake on the plate and felt hunger pangs in his stomach. The scent was as sweet as ever, but somehow he felt like an intruder, as if she didn't really want him to stay.

"Not hungry," he whispered, and turned away.

"We'll be in the cowshed on time," he heard her say, but he didn't reply. Why would they come to the cowshed anyway? He was back on his feet now; he'd take care of the cows like he'd always done. He didn't need any help.

He limped out and for a brief moment he really wanted to slam the door shut behind him. But he didn't.

He was angry, but there was no particular reason for his anger; nobody had done him any wrong—on the contrary. He suddenly realized that Emily had loved him like a true mother, cared for him like no one else had ever done before, and been so kind and understanding. But now she had turned all her affections toward the new boy. Once again, he was alone in the world. And this time it hurt deeply, because now he knew what he had lost.

For days the lava field was wet and gray, and dark clouds marched over the land. Then came a bright day with no wind and a calm ocean. The golden moss sparkled in the sunlight and yellow leaves on bushes in the lava field gleamed. In the morning there were frost roses on the windowpane, and when the moon appeared, pale in the dark-blue sky, frost sparkled on the Cairn of Christ.

Winter was arriving.

17.

A Boy with a Mouth Full of Words

All the little boys had left. Emily told Henry that she and Ollie had stood in the yard, waving good-bye. She said the little boys had pressed their faces against the bus windows, probably hoping that they'd never see the farm again, or perhaps remembering happy days and joyful moments they'd had here, in spite of everything.

Now the only boys left were Henry, John, and Mark—and Ollie, of course. He hadn't come here through the social system, but rather because his late mother had been Emily's childhood friend. When his mother died he had been taken in by his grandparents, who cared for him as long as they were able. But now they were moving to a nursing home and there was no relative to take care of Ollie. His grandparents had found out that Emily was running a home for boys, and wrote her a letter, asking her to bring up the son of her childhood friend.

"It wasn't a difficult decision to make," Emily told Henry. "Especially when I knew all the other boys were being taken away. What would have been the point of staying here if this angel hadn't arrived?" she added, as if to herself.

Henry didn't dare ask: What of me? What of John and Mark?

He was helping her in the kitchen after dinner. Ollie and the other two were watching television in the living room. Perhaps Emily felt that Henry and John and Mark were too grown up to be in need of her love and attention in the same way Ollie was. Perhaps she was right. Perhaps they should be. Henry didn't know about the others, but he knew what he longed for: Emily's love. He never wanted to be parted from her, the woman who was more his mother than his real mother had ever been. But now it seemed that Ollie was the center of her attention. And Henry felt left out.

It had begun to snow.

The land disappeared under a white sheet for as far as the eye could see. And it continued to snow: sometimes delicate grains, sometimes hail, sometimes large heavy flakes that covered everything in an instant. The footsteps of the wind were weighty; it moaned under its burden and poured the thick mass from its bosom with a tired sigh.

But it was warm in the cowshed. Emily had put an electric heater in there for Henry, since his sickness. And it was probably the increased warmth that brought the dung flies. They irritated him constantly when he was working. They sat on his hands and face, heavy and dazed, yellow and furry. Maybe they also had more dirt to feed on, since he didn't bother to wash the dung canal as thoroughly as before. He didn't care as much about cleanliness in the cowshed.

It was also a long time since he had cleaned himself properly. It didn't matter whether he washed or not anyway; the dirt always came back. Emily brought him clean clothes, but he let them lie on the chair. He just milked the cows, and besides that he slept. There were no sheep anymore: the reverend had sold them. Henry couldn't help feeling a little regret, for feeding the sheep had been a part of his duties. And despite the hateful smell, he had enjoyed their eager bleats when he'd appeared at the door of the sheep shed with his arms full of hay. But now the sheds were empty and silent.

His body went through the motions, his hands did the work that needed to be done; he was still the same old ugly cripple that he'd always been. But inside everything had solidified. The sweet feeling that he had experienced so briefly in the last days of summer had disappeared, buried under the thick snow.

After breakfast each morning John and Mark had to shovel the path to the church so they could continue their work in there, painting the ceiling and the walls. After lunch they spent most of their time in the smithy, making pallets for a moving company in the city. It was a new assignment that the reverend had obtained in order to have some income for the home. The boys were happy with the work, for unlike the slavery in the rock mine, they got their share of every pallet they made. It seemed that the reverend had learned his lesson; he even allowed them to smoke, as long as they did it outside the smithy. Sometimes the reverend stayed in the city for days, only coming back on the weekends. Henry didn't know why he went, and Emily never talked about it.

She came with Ollie every morning to help milk the cows. Somehow that had become the new arrangement, without anyone asking Henry his opinion.

Emily gave Ollie the job of carrying the washing bucket and udder fat from her to Henry as they milked. In between, the boy stroked the cows, patted them on the chin, and said things like, "You poor thing, bless you," in the sympathetic tone of an old man.

Ollie was extremely fond of the cows, scratching them behind their ears, talking to them. Henry closed his ears to Ollie's endless chatting and averted his gaze whenever their eyes met. The cows, on the other hand, were happy with the attention they were getting from this little calf. They shot their tongues eagerly into each nostril, their big eyes beaming with affection as they purred.

Then Ollie would fetch a book from the windowsill. He would climb the fence around Noah's stall, sit on the top board, and lock his toes between the pickets with the book on his knees. Then he would read, haltingly, moving his finger slowly from letter to letter. He read for Emily, the cows, and Henry, and his challenge was to finish a certain number of pages during the milking. But sometimes he had to stop, if the words were too long or he didn't understand their meaning.

"How do you say this?" he would ask, holding up the book and pointing at the word with his finger.

That was the worst part. Henry tried very hard not to come

close to him in case he suddenly asked him a question, but, of course, Ollie couldn't always be avoided.

"What's that?" he once asked, pointing out a page to Henry.

Henry was unable to move away without being too obvious. He was right beside Noah's fence, where Ollie was sitting and leaning forward, holding the book up to Henry's face.

Henry saw only a whirlwind of letters, and that old troll of anxiety clenched its fist and punched his stomach. He stood on the edge of the dung canal with the shovel in his hands. He couldn't run away; the book was right in his face, blocking his path. His only other option was to jump across the canal. He rarely did that because he had slipped on his clubfoot more than once and hit the floor.

He clenched his fingers around the handle of the shovel. His forehead was dripping with sweat and his mouth immediately dried up. Henry was certain he would start to stutter as soon as he opened his mouth. He turned abruptly, pushing his shoulder against the book, and growled: "Ask Emily."

"But I'm asking you," the boy demanded.

So the cowshed was no longer Henry's private place; now it belonged to Ollie, who had taken over with his silly cheerfulness, chatting, and nauseating reading sessions. Why couldn't the worm just read in the house? Why the hell did he have to bring books into the cowshed? Henry sometimes glanced at the stack of books on the windowsill and wondered if he should wash them all to the floor with a powerful spout from the hose, just like he did when there were flies on the glass, before the books had appeared.

Emily even held Ollie's hand when they crossed the yard, and it was not as though Ollie needed the support, for he didn't limp. She patted him like a puppy. It was unbearable to watch. And when Ollie didn't join her in the cowshed she was distracted and in a hurry, as if she just wanted to finish the milking as soon as possible.

Henry could just imagine Ollie sitting on the chair by the stove, Emily making some more cocoa for him as he held the cup in both hands to warm his tiny fingers. Ollie hadn't just taken over the cowshed; now Henry's favorite seat had become Ollie's too.

The darkness grew greater and deeper from one day to the next, the light shorter and thinner, the sun more distant and colder. It sank into the western ocean and bright green streaks of light appeared. As darkness overarched the land, the northern lights danced, changing color all the time, from green to purple, moving in graceful waves like silent surf in the ocean of stars.

Henry wondered what they were, these ghostly bands of light shimmering in the dark silence. Perhaps they were the spirits of the damned, cursed to wander for eternity in the emptiness between heaven and Earth. Yes, the spirits of the damned. And one day he would join them.

He sat under the Gallows in the freezing cold, staring up into the heavenly vault.

The God of Summer had given him the false hope of friendship, only to snatch it away and leave him here, naked and lost in the realm of winter. The God of Winter didn't pretend to be anything other than what he really was, indifferent in the vast realm of space. He was a God of Truth, who poured his darkness over the world and didn't care what mortal men said or thought. And for all he cared, a fallen angel could lie where he had fallen.

18.

The Perfect Escape

It was late afternoon and the truck had arrived to collect the milk containers. Henry lifted the containers up to the platform, where the driver stood and stacked them inside the cooler.

When the truck drove off, Henry noticed Mark, standing by the Cairn of Christ. Neither John nor Mark had spoken to him for a long time. Although the rules at breakfast, lunch, and dinner weren't as strict as before, nobody talked much, except Ollie of course. The boy just couldn't keep quiet. Reverend Oswald didn't seem to mind it, and John was rather fond of the little boy. But Mark never said a word. And neither did Henry.

John had changed since he first arrived. Gone was the arrogance, the haughty attitude, his cool way of being. Ever since he'd been locked up in the attic, John had become a fervent believer. It looked like the reverend's prayer sessions had turned him inside out. Now he sometimes asked the reverend to be allowed to say grace at dinner. His green eyes had become dull and somehow reminded Henry of broken pieces of glass. John seemed to spend much of his spare time in the smithy, carving out small figurines. He had told Ollie that they were chess pieces: Christ, Mary, the apostles, and angels in white, the devil with his host of demons and monsters in black. He had been explaining this to Ollie at dinner, showing him his latest figure, Peter the apostle.

"But if black is the devil, what happens when black wins?" Ollie had asked.

John had become silent for a moment, but then he whispered, "That would be very sad."

Henry hadn't really been listening to their talk, but the tone of John's voice had made him look up. And then he had met Mark's burning eyes, looking straight at Henry as if he was about to scream at him.

And now Mark stood there by the cairn, looking at him across the yard, as if he wanted something. Revenge, perhaps, for turning the bottle over to Emily. Henry felt a sudden chill. Henry had decided to walk to the Gallows; now he wondered if that was such a good idea. Perhaps Mark had evil intentions and would follow him. Then Henry remembered he had beaten up the Brute; he would have no trouble handling Mark. He couldn't help but grin as he glanced back at the boy standing by the cairn.

The sun was distant and cold, almost touching the horizon, and the stars were beginning to appear. He made his way through the thick snowdrifts behind the barn, so he wouldn't be seen from the house, and followed Spine Break Path into the lava field, treading in his footsteps from the day before. When he glanced over his shoulder he saw that Mark was now at the corner of the barn. Mark was obviously coming after him. Henry's face suddenly felt warm; they would fight and he would give Mark a beating he'd never forget.

Henry was panting heavily when he reached the two boulders. He sat down in the snow with his back to the cold rock. Glancing out of the corner of his eye, he saw Mark walking slowly down the path.

The sky was red where the sun had disappeared and the dark grew deeper. Soon the only light would be from the stars and the moon, reflecting on the pure white snow.

But there were lights in the distance, moving ever so slowly on the black ocean: three yellow lights on a freighter.

Henry heard the crunching sound of Mark's footsteps coming closer. He sat by the boulders, staring straight ahead, getting ready to jump up and punch Mark in the face, when a distant tone from a foghorn echoed through the frozen air. It was a sad sound of regret, the long drawn wailing sound of a broken heart, saying good-bye for the last time. When the foghorn fell silent at last, Henry noticed that the crunching sound had stopped as well. He turned to look and saw Mark standing still in the dusk, staring at the horizon with searching eyes. The long black body of the freighter could barely be seen; one more blow of the foghorn and it would disappear into darkness.

"Did you hear that?" Mark whispered in a trembling voice.

He moved closer and sat down by Henry's side, shivering from the cold.

"Wait; they'll blow it again in a minute," he said, and lit a cigarette.

They sat in silence for a long moment, side by side, gazing over the ocean.

The freighter was dissolving in the mist. Henry tried to focus on the body of the ship. Then the last tone from the foghorn sounded, so far away they could barely hear it.

"Do you know where it's going?" Mark asked.

Henry shook his head.

"To the Continent," Mark said. "To Germany or Holland, maybe to Spain. Imagine." He sighed, leaning his head back. "In a few days' time the crew will have reached a warm, sunny beach. And you can do anything you want there. Jesus, I want to go to Spain. They've got sun and summer all year round. One day," he said, "one day I'll go there and I'll never come back. If only I could get on that ship."

He blew into his fists to warm them up and rested his eyes on the faraway horizon.

"Spain, man," Mark sighed. "Guys like us could have a good time there," he said, and chuckled. "We could find a good job over there and earn some money. And when we had enough we could go someplace else, or do whatever we wanted." He flashed a smile.

Henry felt strange. Suddenly it was as if they had always been friends, not enemies. Henry was relaxed sitting here beside Mark, listening to him talk. Perhaps Mark wasn't so bad after all; perhaps he only wanted to be Henry's friend.

Henry wanted him to go on talking; he barely felt the cold anymore. But Mark was silent now, gazing toward the horizon. Henry cleared his throat and tried to speak clearly as he timidly asked, "How can you get on board?"

"Well, the plan was to sneak off to the city, go to the harbor, and hide on board one of the freighters," Mark said. "But it's impossible. There's no way we could make it to the city before we're found out."

They sat for a long time, looking at the stars sparkling overhead, each sunk in his own thoughts. Henry suddenly realized that Mark had actually let him in on a secret: Mark was planning an escape for himself and John.

"You know, I really hated you for telling on us," Mark suddenly said. "But when I thought about it, I guess I couldn't blame you." He paused and lit another cigarette. "I'm really sorry," he whispered. "I'm sorry I was such a jerk not inviting you. I thought the girls would be frightened of you and leave."

Henry couldn't reply. There was a sudden lump in his throat.

"It was all lies, you know," Mark continued. "What they said to their parents and the police. We didn't touch them. Neither of us. I guess they just needed to blame someone when they got home so late."

He was silent for a while. Henry felt strangely relieved, listening to Mark. And to his surprise he felt secure somehow, with him by his side. Maybe this was how it felt to have a real friend.

"I'll tell you something," Mark continued. "When I was locked up this summer, Reverend Oswald came in every other day to make me say prayers. He was going to rinse the devil out of me, or something. The only thing I could do was to pretend to be listening and babble those prayers; you have to play along if you don't want to lose your mind," he added, looking inquisitively at Henry.

"And then I sometimes thought about you," he said, squinting his eyes. "I thought: either this guy's an idiot or he's playing that game too."

Henry felt a little uneasy, but Mark put a hand on his arm.

"It's OK, Henry. I know you're not an idiot. I'm just saying, I wish I hadn't treated you like one."

It was as if their mutual hatred in the past made honesty possible now, for hatred is also a sure sign of respect. And now that John was saved and barely spoke with him anymore, Mark had no one else to turn to. Both of them had relied on John's friendship; Henry had lost John to Mark, and now Mark had lost John to Jesus.

Mark stared out at the dark ocean, frowning.

"The only thing that keeps me going is the thought of escape," he whispered. "If I only knew how to get on board a freighter, I'd leave right away and take John with me. Have you seen how he's become? A shadow of himself, that's what he is. If I could just get him out of here, away from this damn country, away from this damn cold," he said, and shivered.

Mark hadn't called him a friend, but he had talked to him like a friend, like someone he trusted. And he had told him a secret. Henry could so easily tell Emily everything, that Mark was planning an escape. Mark knew this; after all, Henry had told on him and John before. Despite that, Mark trusted him now, like a real friend. Henry felt a strange tingling in his stomach, for he suddenly realized that he had something to give his new friend, something that would be of immense value to Mark.

"Th-there's a b-boat," Henry whispered into the frozen silence.

Mark turned his head with a questioning look.

"What?"

"In the s-smithy," Henry said. "A real boat."

Henry moved the wooden barrels that stood by the gable wall. Behind them was the boat, covered with green sailcloth. He rolled one barrel to the side and pulled at the sailcloth. And the boat was revealed, as if by magic.

"Jesus Christ," Mark said with a gasp.

He stood still for a long time, examining the boat with flushed cheeks and gleaming eyes, as if he had witnessed a heavenly revelation.

Henry stood behind him, smiling to himself.

He might have lost Emily to the new boy, but he had made a friend of his worst enemy. And that was no small achievement.

Suddenly the days had acquired a new meaning, a new purpose. Each morning Henry woke up excited, constantly thinking about where and when they would meet again to talk about the big secret.

He was impatient to finish the milking so he could get rid of Ollie and Emily from the cowshed, in case Mark came to talk. He couldn't help becoming irritated by Ollie when he lingered in the cowshed after milking. Henry would take the hose, turn on the water, and start to wash the floor and the dung canal so the water sprayed in every direction. That usually did the trick, and the boy left with a sour face.

They never arranged any of their meetings, but when the weather was fine and there was still some daylight they met at the Gallows. They'd sit there, side by side, refining the escape plan.

It was usually Mark who did most of the talking, but sometimes they barely exchanged any words at all. Occasionally Henry was the first to say something, and he felt compelled to reply if Mark asked him something, but speaking wasn't as hard as he had imagined. Sometimes he even managed to come out with a complete sentence without stuttering, because Mark didn't press him, but waited patiently and listened.

And, day by day, the perfect escape plan began to take form. The freighters always sailed the same route, just like buses. They followed signals from the shore until they reached the international sea routes. That's how it had to be.

The problem was: how do you jump on a bus in the middle of the ocean?

Henry had no answer to that.

"You sail in front of it," Mark explained, "and let the boat glide by its side. Then you fasten the hook on the ladder."

"What ladder?" Henry asked.

"There's an iron ladder down its side. It's soldered on," Mark said.

"They sail too fast," Henry said skeptically.

"Too fast?" Mark cried. "They sail at twenty knots!"

Henry gave him a questioning look.

"That's slow," Mark said. "It's a piece of cake," he added, squinting at the horizon.

The only real problem that troubled Mark was how to move the little boat from the smithy into the water. There was no beach, only tall cliffs in both directions. Mark thought it was, in fact, ridiculous to have a boat here in the first place, because there was no way to put it to sea.

But Henry told him the story of the farmer, whom the neighbors had nicknamed the Miracle Man. Then he explained the wheel he had found in the smithy, and the iron bar that was drilled into the cliff. The wheel and the iron bar were obviously a part of the mechanism that the Miracle Man had used to lower the boat down the cliffs onto the sandbank when the tide was low.

But they couldn't try this out until they had moved the boat to the cliffs. And for the time being that was impossible, because they needed a third man. Mark would have to convince John, somehow, to help them, and hopefully to join them.

Mark obviously considered Henry to be on the team. After all, he had found the boat. And Spain awaited them, with its sunny beaches, right on the other side of the horizon. Henry felt proud to be a member of the mission and imagined it wouldn't be that hard to hook the ladder on the side of the ship.

"We'll only get one shot at it though," Mark said.

Henry nodded with a pensive air. He could see that it would be difficult, of course, but he felt he was up to the task.

"I'll keep the boat steady while you do it," Mark said. "If we only had a motor on the boat, it would make things a lot easier."

"No," Henry said with a professional air. "They'd hear the noise."

"You're right," Mark said.

Of course, the ingenious part of the plan, Mark thought, was to be on a rowboat and to float up to the side of the freighter without a sound. They rehearsed this in their minds over and over again, pondering any problems and imagining their actions from every conceivable angle.

"A freighter like that is pretty steady on the water," Mark said. "It might even work to our advantage if there were some waves. But, of course, the risk is less if the ocean is still."

Henry agreed; large waves would raise the boat up by the freighter's side and make it easier to hook on to the ladder. He had begun to accept the fact that this would be his mission on the journey.

"There's no way we can fail," Mark said. "We climb aboard, hide somewhere in a container, and sit pretty. And then we're on our way to Spain," he added.

"Into the sun," Henry said with a broad smile.

He didn't worry that his smile looked like a mocking scowl or that it revealed his crooked teeth. He trusted his former enemy completely to understand his expression the way he really meant it.

19.

The "Poem of the Sun"

On days when temperatures fell well below zero, Henry sometimes noticed Ollie walking around the yard, scattering bread-
crumbs for the little birds that flocked in the sky. Then he'd
run around a corner, waiting for them to gather for the feast.
Within moments, they dived down from the sky in their hundreds, pecking at the snow with their tiny beaks. Ollie would
try to move closer to examine them better, but they were wary
little creatures. Ollie only had to take one step toward them
and they all flew up in the same instant, scattering in large
black clouds with a sudden flutter of their tiny wings. They
twirled toward the sky in a long arch, either stretching apart or
bundling tightly together, a hundred tiny bodies sharing one
big soul. Ollie stood in the middle of the yard, following them
with his eyes: the great soul-cloud of the birds dancing on the
frosty white morning.

Henry had now become used to having Ollie in the cowshed. He didn't mind if Ollie was reading; actually it was quite
nice to listen to his voice while milking. His presence had
ceased to be a threat, especially now that Henry and Mark had
become friends. Sometimes Henry went to the smithy after

milking and helped John and Mark with the pallets. Mark had decided that the time still wasn't right to reveal the boat to John. Perhaps Mark hadn't made up his mind about rescuing John, Henry thought. Perhaps Mark was worried about whether John could be trusted, now that he was saved and all that. Maybe he would go straight to the reverend and then all would be for nothing. The only thing John seemed interested in was his carving. He spent long hours sitting at a table in the smithy with his chess pieces and a sharp knife.

One day in the cowshed, Ollie was watching the dung flies on the windowpane. When the light fell on the glass, they gathered on the same spot, cramming on top of one another, following the sunbeam right up to the corner of the window until it faded and disappeared.

"Look, Henry," he said. "See how the flies follow the sunbeam on the glass. I wonder why they do that?"

Henry had no idea and didn't reply. He thought that as the flies were gathered in a bunch, the boy could exterminate them once and for all.

"Maybe they live on the sun," Ollie said, "and are trying to get back home. What do you think of that, Henry? Maybe they're old sunbeams that have shed their light. That's why they have to get back home to the sun, don't you see? To become bright and glowing again and to fly all over and shine again!" he said, watching the flies with affection.

Henry had tried hard to exterminate the flies in the cowshed, but now that Ollie thought he'd discovered their purpose— that they were in fact burned-out sunbeams on their way home to regain their light—Henry felt a sudden longing to help them fulfill their destiny.

Another evening, when the northern lights twirled in the starry sky, Ollie stopped in the doorway of the cowshed, awestruck, looking up at the magnificent spectacle in the dark sky.

"Look," he whispered. "The Lord of Winter charges on with his chariot." He pointed his tiny finger at the northern lights.

Henry didn't reply, but Ollie smiled mysteriously, as if he was telling him a secret not many people knew.

"He has twelve ice-horses that pull his chariot across the sky," Ollie said.

Henry snorted and shook his head.

"The northern lights," Ollie explained, "are the hoof dust of the ice-horses, pulling the Lord of Winter's chariot."

Henry glanced at the northern lights.

"Hoof dust? What's that?"

"It's the magical dust from the horses' hooves," Ollie said in a mysterious whisper. "It's the dust that all beautiful dreams are made from."

When Ollie had left, Henry stood for a long time, watching the heavenly journey of the Lord of Winter on his chariot. The mysterious hoof dust from the ice-horses clearly showed how fast the Lord of Winter traveled. Henry remembered having decided that the lights were the souls of the damned, but not anymore. It was strange how Ollie's thoughts and words could change everything into magic and wonder.

Ollie talked a lot about his grandparents. They had taught him hundreds of old rhymes and poetry of all sorts. Sometimes

Henry had a hard time holding back his laughter when the boy recited a poem at the dinner table, putting on a serious frown like an old man; even his voice sounded old.

Ollie had a special way of measuring distances; he measured them in poems and rhymes, like his grandfather had taught him. For instance, there was one poem that could circle the Cairn of Christ three times, he told Henry with a triumphant smile. Another poem stretched all the way around the barn. Then there was one that covered the exact distance between the house and the garage door. Sometimes Henry saw him stopping abruptly in the middle of the yard, tilting his head and looking very thoughtful. Ollie explained to Henry that he was unable to move any farther because the poem had ended in the middle of the yard and he had to search his mind for another one to be able to continue his walk.

Emily followed him everywhere with sweaters and woolen socks, but he couldn't stand wearing warm clothes and always pulled them off, either in the cowshed or in the yard, and then forgot where he'd left them. Warm clothes simply got in his way, especially coats or scarfs. And there was no way Emily could get him to wear warm boots and socks; he complained his feet were suffocating. The most he would wear were his old moccasins with no socks.

One evening Ollie didn't show up for dinner. It was freezing outside and pitch-dark. The reverend was away, so Henry and Mark went out with Emily searching for him. Emily had become frightened and called loudly, her voice echoing in the yard. Finally they heard a tiny voice out in the lava field. They found Ollie standing by the church, where he said he couldn't move from. He hadn't been able to remember the next verse of the "Poem of the Sun." It was the one that reached all the way back to the house, but he was stuck where he was, racking his brain, for it would have been cheating to repeat the same verse to get back.

"You must never do that again," Emily demanded sternly.

But Ollie gave her a strange look and said, "I have to measure everything with poems. It's very important."

"Why is it important?" Emily said, throwing her hands in the air.

"Because then, everything will be all right. Then, nothing bad can happen," he said in a thin voice, and lowered his head. "And the 'Poem of the Sun' is the best poem there is," he added. "You'll never get lost if you know the 'Poem of the Sun.'"

After that he caught a cold and had to stay in bed, so Emily turned up for milking on her own, looking worried, irritated and impatient. And she often left before it was finished.

When Henry was scraping the dung canal or the roof beams creaked from the wind, he thought for a moment he heard Ollie's bright and cheerful voice ringing through. He glanced at the fence around Noah's stall, where Ollie had sat so often with the books on his lap, and felt a surprising pang of regret that he wasn't there.

Henry remembered some of the silly things Ollie had said, and he laughed out loud. It surprised him how hard he could laugh once he'd started. It was peculiar to hear one's own laughter in the cowshed.

"When I grow up I want to be a grandfather," Ollie once said.

"You'll have to become a father first," Emily replied.

"Why?"

"It's the law of life."

"Then I'll break the law and do what I want."

The giggle burst out of Henry without warning. It was a nice feeling, this tickling deep inside, triggered by the little worm's silly words and strange thoughts.

Henry entered the kitchen with the milk container and heard Emily's voice from upstairs. She was reading to Ollie because he couldn't fall asleep without having a story read to him.

After two visits from the doctor, Ollie was back on his feet again. He came to the cowshed, climbed up on Noah's fence, and watched them milk the cows. He had a book on his knees. But he couldn't read for long, because he said his eyes were tired. He was also too tired to pat the cows or comb them, so he watched Henry do it instead when Emily was gone.

"Will you read for me?" Ollie said with a sigh.

The blizzard outside was so wet and heavy that you could barely see your hands in front of your face. The beams creaked loudly as the storm pounded the roof.

"Henry? Will you read for me?" he begged.

Henry continued brushing Old Red and acted as if he hadn't heard him. But Ollie wasn't going to give up. He climbed down from the fence, placed himself on the other side of Old Red, and put the open book on her back, right in front of Henry.

"Someone has to read for me," he said almost as an order, wrinkling his brows.

"Why?" Henry said.

"I must have a story today. If I don't I might as well die," was the honest reply.

"Ask Emily."

"She hasn't the time today."

"Neither have I," Henry growled, turning away.

He threw the comb away and tried to think of something to do to show Ollie how busy he was. Emily hadn't washed the milk buckets, so he grabbed the yellow hose, turned the water on, and began to clean them. He made sure that the water sprayed all around him and in Ollie's direction. The buckets rang loudly as he split the jet of water with his thumb.

He hoped, prayed even, that Ollie would lose his patience and leave. But he stood still with a stubborn look on his face and waited so that he could continue to plead.

He couldn't wash the buckets forever so he pointed the jet at the dung canal, pretending he needed to clean it more thoroughly. Ollie retreated two steps from the water. It was a kind of game, Henry thought. Now was the moment to see which of them had the most stamina.

"You are my brother, and older brothers are supposed to be kind," Ollie said.

Henry bent the hose and choked the stream.

"Huh? I'm not your brother."

"But you've got to read for me," the boy said, and his voice was breaking.

"I do?"

"Yes. I read for you when you were sick," he said, holding the book out to him. "And now my eyes are too tired, so you must do it for me. Please."

Henry turned off the water, faced the wall, and started to wind up the hose in slow motion while he tried to think up an answer. He was panicking now.

"Well, I wasn't listening," he finally snapped.

The door slammed behind him.

On a nail by the door hung Ollie's coat and scarf. The stormy wind howled overhead and the roof creaked more loudly. Henry wiped the mist off the windowpane and looked out.

Ollie was standing out there in the blizzard, squeezing his book against his chest, looking around him, as if he had lost his way and didn't know the direction to the house. He was like a tiny bird that had lost its flock and didn't know where to find them. Ollie took a step into the whiteness and disappeared. Henry flung the door open, but the blizzard struck him so hard in the face he had to turn away to catch his breath.

Serves him right, Henry thought, slamming the door. Serves him right, not wearing a coat in a blizzard like this. It would only be fair if he caught a cold or pneumonia or something. Yeah, serves him right for talking like that, Henry decided, like Henry had done him some injustice or something.

Still Henry waited by the window to see if Ollie appeared again. After a while he took the coat and the scarf and pushed himself out into the blizzard, heading for the house.

He thought at least if he took the clothes with him, Emily wouldn't have a reason to scold Ollie for leaving them.

When he entered the kitchen he saw Ollie's book lying on the table. And from upstairs he heard Emily's soothing voice through Ollie's sobbing. Henry felt bad for having hurt him. But how could he explain to the boy that his dearest passion was also Henry's greatest fear?

20.
Holy Night

Christmas approached with pitch-black darkness and a snowstorm. Everyone participated in the preparations under Emily's command. Mark and Henry wrestled against the tempest, trying to fasten lights on the mountain ash outside the living-room window. Ollie and John had fun cutting out figures in the cinnamon dough, while Reverend Oswald sat by the stove and watched, sipping coffee. From the radio in the living room the Christmas carols found their way around the house; Emily seemed to know all the songs by heart.

Every night Ollie put a moccasin in the window. Each morning he sat up in bed and examined the snow outside. There were no footprints. And yet there were sweets from Santa in the shoe. He asked everyone how Santa had managed to put the sweets there, for the house had no chimney. Did he have a key to every house? Or could he, perhaps, walk through walls? If so, was Santa a ghost? Or did he have magic? If he had magic, then why didn't he just make the candy appear in every house, instead of walking across the country each and every night till Christmas with a sack full of sweets?

There were no easy answers to all his questions.

On Christmas Eve Emily set the dining-room table while John and Mark played cards in the living room, and Henry and Ollie watched cartoons on the television.

Reverend Oswald sat down with the boys, trying to find something to talk about. But they were a little shy. It was only Ollie who spoke and wanted to know if the reverend had met Santa. Oswald just smiled and gave no clear answers.

Emily laid the food on the table, and everyone sat down. Oswald said a long prayer, and then they all said the Lord's Prayer together. Ollie's voice chimed brightly as always, John recited it devoutly, with a serious look on his face, and even Mark and Henry mumbled along, for it was Christmas after all.

After dinner the reverend cleared the table while Emily played the piano. Ollie stood by her side and sang "Silent Night" in his clear, bright voice.

Each of the boys got a soft parcel from the couple: woolen mittens, a sweater, and a scarf.

John got a present from his parents: a wood-carving set in a hardwood box with razor-sharp knives and tiny chisels, well-made steel instruments. It looked expensive. Henry noticed that a tear ran down John's cheek, and he wiped it away quickly so no one would notice. But Henry did and wondered why this strange present had made him so sad. After all, he was a skilled carver, so he should be happy to get a professional carving set. Maybe it had been a happy tear?

Henry got a present from his mother: a pair of fine leather gloves and five pairs of socks. Henry tried the gloves on and thought perhaps he would use them when he was pushing the wheelbarrow.

Mark only got a card from his aunt, who was trying to make up for his father's negligence. There was cash in the card for him to buy something nice with. Mark laughed and asked where on earth he was going to buy anything. But the reverend promised that as soon as the roads were clear he would take Mark to a shop in the village.

Ollie got a tiny farm from his aging grandparents, with little animals and a tractor. He disappeared into his game on the living-room floor, and everyone else settled down in their seats. Emily continued to play the piano, and Oswald read a book. Henry noticed that John just sat with his tool kit in his lap, tapping his fingers on the wooden box.

Before Henry went to bed he gave the cows an extra portion of hay for a Christmas treat. He felt good after the meal with the gravy and the caramel potatoes and fell asleep as soon as his head hit the pillow.

But he hadn't slept for long when the door to his room was flung open so hard it hit the wall with a loud bang. He sat up with his heart thumping in his chest, but the room was dark. Then suddenly Mark appeared by his bedside, his face pale in the moonlight, his eyes big as saucers.

"Help me! Come quickly!" he gasped, and tore at Henry's arm, dragging him out of bed.

Henry followed Mark to the dormitory where he and John slept. Henry had never been in there before. All around the room were empty bunk beds where Henry guessed the little ones had slept. But now they were like graves inside a murky tomb, except where John sat, hunched forward. The wind howled over the roof. Henry felt his heart drumming loudly in his ears and he took a deep breath.

The lamp by John's bed cast an arc of light on the floorboards. John had a knife in his hand and was staring into the darkness; blood was dripping from his wrist, forming a dark pool on the wooden floorboards.

It took Henry a moment to realize what had happened. Mark edged slowly toward John, and Henry followed.

John sniffed. He seemed to be looking at them from far away.

"Who are you?"

Mark stood still for a while, but Henry tried to figure out how they could stop him from hurting himself more. If they were careful they might be able to take the knife from him.

"It's me. Mark. And Henry is here too. Don't be afraid," Mark whispered.

"They wanted me to kill myself," John whispered, sobbing. "My parents, I mean. Why didn't they take me home for Christmas? Why did they send me these knives? I will go to hell for this," he said with trembling lips as he looked at the bleeding wound on his wrist. "I don't want to go to hell! Please, help me, please." His voice broke and tears flowed down his cheeks.

"You'll be all right," Mark whispered.

He sat down beside John and carefully placed his hand on the knife.

John stared at the knife for a long moment before releasing his hold. The blood gushed out of the wound on his other wrist.

Mark took the knife gently from his hand then quickly cut a strip off his T-shirt. He took the wounded arm in his hand and wrapped the strip tightly around John's bleeding wrist.

John looked at him, his troubled eyes searching Mark's face for an answer or an explanation of some kind. Mark tried to smile.

"We are your friends," he whispered. "Henry and I. And we're going away from here soon, I promise you. All three of us. So don't you worry about a thing."

A shy, trusting smile appeared on John's lips. Tears ran from his eyes and his breath trembled.

"Will you stay with me?" he pleaded.

"I will," Mark replied.

John fumbled for Mark's hand and lay back. Then he sighed, closed his eyes, and fell asleep in an instant.

Mark sat on the bed for a long time, holding the bandage tightly on John's wounded arm while the weather pounded the roof, the beams creaked, and the wind howled.

Henry sat on the other bed and waited.

"Will he be all right?" he whispered.

"He has to be," Mark said. "We just have to take good care of him, you and I. As soon as we can, we must move the boat to the cliffs."

"As soon as winter is through, we're gone," he whispered.

Looking at John sleeping, Henry wondered if it was such

a good idea anymore. John was desperate enough to attempt suicide, and so Mark seemed more determined than ever to save his friend. To save him from Jesus, and the reverend, from his parents, from his criminal record, and this cold country that offered no hope for the future, but only more trouble.

Back in his own room, Henry wondered what it was that Mark wanted to escape from so badly. Was it just the farm? It wasn't really so bad here. Or was it something else? Henry knew one thing for certain, for it had been the story of his life; nobody could escape from himself. And the more he thought about it, the more he realized that Mark had probably not learned that lesson.

21.

A Miracle in the Smithy

The first two months of the New Year, as always, were utter darkness. Snow covered everything, and it was as if time had come to a full stop. There were no days, only eternal night. Henry woke up in darkness and went to bed in darkness and between that, nothing happened.

Every morning the snow had once again covered the tracks he trod between the cowshed and the house, so when he finally reached the farmhouse, he was fuming inside and wanted to scream at everyone.

Ollie had the flu and so the breakfast table was quiet. Emily stayed by Ollie's bedside and Henry milked alone. Henry found himself hearing Ollie's voice every time the shovel scraped the canal or when the wind pounded the roof. Words here and there, sometimes whole sentences, began to reverberate in his head, in that ringing clear voice, reading a story or chanting an ancient poem.

Henry put on the leather gloves from his mom, fought his way through a snowdrift with the wheelbarrow full of steaming shit, and emptied it onto the frozen dung heap.

Sometimes, while he worked, Henry thought about what

Reverend Oswald had said about agricultural college, so long ago. Although it was almost unbelievable that it would ever happen, he allowed himself the luxury of dreaming.

He imagined a beautiful countryside with green fields as far as the eye could see and no lava fields, a cowshed full of happy fat cows, and a brand-new dairy machine. Maybe even horses too.

But it was just a dream; he knew that. Emily did not force him to read, and he did not want to, so it would all come to nothing. He would never be allowed into college. Why on earth did farmers have to read anyway? Farmers worked with their hands and took care of their animals. Books didn't have anything to do with that.

Henry guessed he would stay here for the rest of his life, unless he ran away with Mark and John. He'd been excited about the idea, though mostly he'd been excited about Mark becoming his friend. But all they ever talked of was the escape plan and how Mark imagined life in Spain. Mark never asked Henry about how *he* felt about it, what *his* dreams were. And as the weeks went by, Henry found himself being more of a listener than a participant. He was the audience that Mark needed to think out loud to, to paint his dream for so he could see it more clearly himself.

Mark was worried about John, who had been in bed since Christmas. Emily had asked the doctor to have a look at him. Mark told John to say that he had cut himself in the smithy. Whether the doctor believed it or not, he realized that John was depressed, so he prescribed some pills for him.

Finally, thanks to Mark's encouragement, John got out of bed and began to fiddle about with wood in the smithy again. Now he sat there every day carving out his chess pieces.

"The sooner I get him away from here, the better," Mark said.

Henry sat by Mark's side but said nothing. In his mind he played with the idea that if John and Mark went to Spain, he would probably be allowed to drive the tractor next summer. He would mow the fields on his own and fill up the barn with fresh hay. And perhaps he would teach Ollie to milk the cows, herd them to pasture, and take care of them since he would be far too busy himself. Thinking of that made him feel better. But at the same time he felt guilty because Mark relied on him for the escape plan.

Every time they talked, Henry couldn't help thinking how much he would miss the farm, the cows, Emily and Ollie, maybe even the reverend. What would he do in Spain, anyway? But he dared not say anything to Mark. Perhaps they weren't real friends after all. You should be able to say anything to a friend. Maybe they were just talking because Mark needed Henry's friendship even more than Henry needed Mark's. Mark needed someone to help him escape to that faraway place where dreams came true. But Henry knew that his dreams were right here, waiting for him in the summer breeze.

The rain showers arrived from the ocean and the snow melted into the lava. One day a green knoll of moss appeared from under the snow and the southern winds rounded up the fluffy clouds and made them gallop across the sky.

The promise of spring laughed in a brook and whispered in the yellow grass at the swamp. It shook the ptarmigan in flight with a playful gust of wind, which made it spring into the air, brown-breasted and white-winged.

Then the birds arrived at the sea cliffs.

The wind was warm and the foxes' cackles echoed across the lava field. The ocean was wild with joy. The surf foamed like mad around the cliffs, gushing up from crevices and clefts in high fountains that collapsed on the rocks with loud smacks.

Now that spring had arrived, Mark was tackling the escape plan with new energy. He was eager for a chance to move the boat to the cliffs, but they couldn't do that in broad daylight unless the reverend and Emily went away. But they could sneak down to the sea cliffs and try out Henry's idea with the iron bar and the wheel with the long steel cable. They carried the wheel out of the smithy between them and hid it behind the barn. After dinner one night they carried it down Spine Break Path, past the Gallows, and continued all the way to the edge of the cliffs above Shipwreck Bay. The iron bar fit perfectly into the square hole in the middle of the wheel.

The end of the cable should obviously be fastened to the hook on the stern of the boat. That way one person could lower the boat down the cliffs, turning the wheel slowly, while another held on to the chain, making sure the boat didn't get stuck on the way down. It was simple, once they had figured it out.

But they still had to wait for a chance to carry the boat out to the cliffs to test this properly. Meanwhile Mark decided it was time to let John in on the plan.

When Henry got to the smithy, John sat by the table with his chess pieces in front of him. He was explaining to Mark that the white pieces were Christ the King and Queen Mary, his mother. There were archangels instead of bishops, knights, and castles, and the pawns were all apostles. The King of Darkness and the Queen of Lust made up the black team, with all kinds of demons and goblins as their bishops, knights, and pawns.

"Soon we'll be able to play chess, Mark," John said with a smile. "It'll be a great battle when these two meet," he added, raising a half-finished Christ and a fully-fledged King of Darkness.

Mark took a piece in his hand and examined it.

"It looks good," he said.

"That's Andrew the apostle," John explained. "He's the brother of Peter," he added, pointing at another figure holding a key.

"What's Andrew holding?" Mark asked.

"Oh, it's supposed to be a net," John said, frowning. "But it's not very clear."

"Oh, right. He was a sailor, wasn't he?" Mark asked.

"A fisherman," John replied. "The Savior's fisherman."

"Must be fun being a fisherman, don't you think?" Mark said. "Sailing the ocean on a little boat? Would you like that?"

"Yeah, but we don't have a boat," John replied.

"But what if we had one?" Mark continued. "Then we could go fishing."

John looked down and chipped a tiny fragment off Christ's shoulder with his knife.

"Yes, but we can't be fishermen if we don't have a boat," he mumbled, and seemed to become immersed in his work again.

Mark watched him for a moment.

Then he walked toward the wall, moved the barrels away, and rolled them across the floor. John looked up slowly, watching his friend with surprise.

"I tell you, brother," Mark said, "the Lord will provide."

Grabbing the corner of the sailcloth, Mark pulled it away in one swift movement, causing dust to scatter in the air around him.

John put Christ down on the table and stood up, gawking at the rowboat. The dust twisting and turning in the air, catching the light from the bright sunbeams pouring through the window, caused the boat to glow in a heavenly light.

"It's a sign," he whispered.

He walked toward the boat, touching it gently, as if he were afraid it would disappear as easily as it had appeared if he weren't careful. But it was a real boat, a real fisherman's boat. John knelt beside it, stroking it hard as if testing its strength, with a big smile on his face.

"A miracle," he murmured.

"The only thing we have to do," Mark said, "is to move it to the cliffs."

John nodded, mesmerized.

"And then we can sail wherever we want to. Even to Spain," Mark said.

John laughed a little, but then he fell silent and looked at Mark as if he had suddenly understood what he was really talking about. "I'd like that," he whispered finally.

A few weeks passed until a day came when Emily decided she had to take Ollie to the city to buy him new clothes. At breakfast the reverend told the boys to keep up the good work in the smithy and said they would be back before dinnertime. As soon as the car had disappeared down the road, Henry emptied the last bucket of milk into a container. Then he hurried to the smithy, where the other two were waiting.

The rusty hinges creaked loudly as Henry pushed the double doors open. Mark and John turned the boat and dragged it between them out into the yard. There was a fresh southerly wind; the sun was bright between the light clouds. Now and then a few large drops fell from the sky as if it was about to rain. But the wind grabbed the curtains of showers and threw them north across the red slopes of the mountains.

After several failed attempts to lift the boat and carry it, they decided to turn it over. Mark slid one oar under it, which John grabbed on the other side. That way they were able to lift the stern. Henry placed himself under the bow, letting it rest on his shoulder.

As he limped onward, they followed. They inched their

way across the yard with the boat on their shoulders, along Spine Break Path. They had to stop many times on the way to rest, especially Henry. His foot ached under the weight of the boat.

Gray curtains moved past the sun and heavy drops smacked the hull of the boat. As the rain showers glided across the lava field, glowing rainbows appeared in their wake.

When they finally reached the cliffs, a wave broke, lashing white foam around the rusty wreck of *Young Hope*. A little farther out the sea was calmer. The timing was right. The tide was low. They had four hours before it would begin to rise.

They rolled the wheel into place and fit it on the iron bar. Then they pulled the end of the cable and locked it to the iron ring on the stern of the boat. Henry rotated the wheel slowly while Mark and John eased the boat carefully over the edge.

The iron wheel squeaked as Henry unwound the cable. The boat drifted slowly down the cliff wall, but Mark hung on to the chain by the steps, supporting it with one hand. The white birds screeched all around them, astonished to see a boat sailing down the cliffs.

Henry clung to the rusty chain, following John down the steps. When they had reached the sandbank below, they pushed the boat into the water and stepped on board. It rocked sideways, light on the waves. Mark put out the oars and practiced rowing.

John just gazed up at the birds on the cliffs, spellbound.

Once they were out of the bay, Mark turned the boat westward.

From here the cliffs seemed to rise much higher than Henry had imagined.

Monstrous rock formations rose from the deep, reaching higher and higher to places that no one could reach but the bird on the wing. The birds seemed so tiny as they spun in an endless whirlpool, like snowflakes spiraling around the cliff wall.

A single bird followed the boat for a while in silent observation. The joyful sound of its beating wings rapidly approached and then faded into the distance.

The day was pink and fresh, and clattering sounds echoed from gorges and peaks above them, across the silvered surface. The waves barely rose before sinking again to the rhythm of the ocean's slow and silent breaths.

John smiled.

"It's a good life, being a fisherman," Mark said.

"It sure is," John said. "It's perfect freedom."

His eyes were shimmering again.

Henry glanced at Mark. His determined look gave nothing away, but Henry knew that he would go through with the plan, now that John had more or less agreed to it. The escape had been set in motion; there was no turning back now. In a week or two they would be boarding a freighter out on the open sea, heading for freedom, out there somewhere, where dreams came true.

Mark turned the boat and headed back to Shipwreck Bay, the boat gliding past the wreck of *Young Hope*. He pulled in the oars as they looked up at the wreck.

It was much larger than it seemed from the edge. It looked like a rusty red whale carcass, with broken ribs jabbing the sky, its portholes like hollow eyes.

From the gaping wound lay chains and wires like rotting intestines, all tangled up with long blades of seaweed that rose and sank in the slow waves with a heavy sigh. As the undercurrent moved the boat toward the bank, John stretched out his hand so his fingertips brushed gently along the rust-burned carcass.

They pulled the boat up the cliffs, but there was no place there to hide it properly. So they raised it upon their shoulders and carried it toward the Gallows. They put it down behind the two boulders, where it was invisible from the farmyard.

They didn't speak on their way back. The next time they walked Spine Break Path would be the last time.

22.

A Sudden Silence

Ollie was out and about again, measuring the important distances around the farm with poems. It was a project he took very seriously; Henry couldn't understand why, but there was much he didn't understand about Ollie. The way he thought, the things he talked about, how all of a sudden he could burst into a song without any reason at all, just because he felt like it.

Henry had noticed that he wasn't the only one being neglected by Emily because of Ollie. Reverend Oswald seemed somehow to have fallen into a shadow. A lot of things had changed, now that there wasn't a big group of boys anymore. The reverend spent most of his time at the farm in his office. Occasionally Henry saw him walking to the new church, perhaps to check if the windows were tightly shut or to sweep dead flies off the windowsills.

He had decided on a date for the first service in the new church, and had invited all the people in the area to come. He spent his days out walking, preparing his sermon, or so he said. And he continued to drive off to the city for days on end, without returning.

Emily didn't seem to mind. Henry knew she had moved Ollie to her bedroom when he caught the flu, and since then the reverend had slept in the Boiler Room. Even though Ollie was fine now, they hadn't changed things back to normal. Early morning when Henry came into the kitchen with the home container full of milk, he heard the reverend's snoring from behind the Boiler Room door. It was as if they had ceased being husband and wife. Ollie and Emily were like mother and child, and it seemed that the reverend had become a guest in his own house.

Sometimes Henry thought about his mother, but it was getting harder for him to remember her face. What was left in his memory were a few moments from his childhood, some of them happy, some of them sad, but her face seemed to escape him. More often than not it was Emily's face that appeared in his mind when he thought of happy things. And then sometimes he got angry, because she was being the kind of mother to Ollie that he himself felt he needed the most. Maybe he was too grown-up for her to behave like a mother to him. Maybe she was afraid of him because he had beaten his mother and broken her arm. But perhaps it was his own fault; if he hadn't thrown her book away, then maybe things would be different now. And if Ollie hadn't arrived? Yes, things would definitely be very different.

Henry put the last shovel of dung in the wheelbarrow and pushed it out. Somewhere behind the barn he could hear Ollie's voice, reciting a poem once again. When he came around the corner Henry saw him walking in his peculiar way, taking long strides very slowly along the wall of the barn, singing out the poem.

Henry emptied the wheelbarrow and wiped his forehead with his arm. Ollie stopped and looked at him.

"You startled me. I forgot the next line," Ollie said.

"Sorry," Henry replied.

"No, wait! What's that? Over there?" Ollie said, pointing at the lava field.

Henry looked at the two boulders.

"The Gallows," he said.

"Where they hanged the thieves and the murderers?" Ollie said, and shivered in horror.

Emily had obviously told him the story. Henry gave him a nod.

"I must go there," Ollie said, suddenly excited. "It is most important!"

"Why?"

"Because bad things happened there," Ollie said. "They need a poem."

"Who?"

"The thieves and the murderers," Ollie said, as if it was obvious. "And of course, all the little children," he added in a lower voice.

So Emily had told him about that too.

"It's important to spread poems over all the places where something bad has happened," Ollie said in a serious tone.

Henry wondered for a moment what on earth had put such a strange idea into his head. Perhaps it was his way of dealing with bad memories, his way to erase the sadness from his mind by performing this strange ritual.

"I know just the right poem," Ollie said with a smile. "It's so long it could reach all the way out there and back again! The 'Poem of the Sun.' It's perfect!"

"You can't," Henry said, and lowered his brows, trying hard to give the impression that he had some authority in the matter.

"Why not?"

That was a harder one. Firstly, if Ollie walked to the Gallows he might see the boat that they had hidden behind the two boulders. Then he'd begin to ask questions or tell Emily about it. Secondly, the pits and crevasses around the boulders were dangerous, and Emily would definitely not allow him to go there on his own.

"It's forbidden. It's dangerous," he replied finally.

But Ollie just smiled, as if he knew very well that Henry wasn't telling the truth.

"But you go there," he said. "I've seen you many times. You and Mark."

This came as a surprise. It probably showed on his face, for Ollie burst out laughing.

"That's different," Henry managed to say, racking his brain to come up with an explanation that Ollie would accept.

"Why?"

" 'Cause we're two. If something happens," he finally said.

"Then you'll come with me," Ollie said, and his face lit up with sheer joy.

But Henry shook his head and grabbed the handles on the wheelbarrow.

"I'm busy," he growled, and limped around the corner. Hopefully this would be enough to keep him away from the lava field, at least for the time being.

Back in the cowshed he could hear Ollie continue his recital behind the barn. That was a relief; he wouldn't dare to go out there on his own.

Time working in the cowshed passed slowly for Henry. He was, once again, left alone with the milking. Now that Ollie was busy with his strange project of measuring the farm in poems, he had no time to hang around the cows, as he put it. Henry was pleased and a little sad as well. After all, he had become used to having Ollie sitting there reading his books, his tiny voice filling the cowshed with words and questions. Yes, now that Ollie was busy with other things, Henry couldn't help feeling a little lonely. And the cows sighed with boredom, mooing, annoyed, as if they missed him as well, the little calf that used to give them so much attention.

That evening, when Henry had filled the home container, he dragged it outside and carried it across the yard. There was a raven sitting upon the Cairn of Christ, looking around as if searching for something. Henry let go of the container, raised his hands in the air, and waved them above his head to scare it off, for the little gray bird with the long black tail had made a nest in the cairn and Henry didn't want the raven to discover it. The raven spread its wings, glided over the yard, and sat on the roof of the barn, croaking loudly as if mocking him. Henry grabbed the container, but then he noticed the silence in the yard. He looked around him, listening, but he heard nothing: no poems, no chirping in the lava, and no distant chatter from the birds in the cliffs, just the rumble of the surf and a gust of wind on his cheeks.

The raven croaked loudly as Henry limped toward the house, dragging the container with him.

Emily was preparing dinner in the kitchen: a spicy goulash with mashed potatoes, Henry's favorite. John was setting the table in the dining room; Mark had just arrived from the village with the reverend. Mark had bought himself a beautiful hunting knife with the money he got at Christmas. It had an ornate handle, a huge blade, and a fine black leather holster. Emily wasn't pleased that Oswald had allowed Mark to buy a knife.

But the reverend said, "Well, boys are fond of knives; it's always been like that." It sounded as if the reverend was trying to make up for the past, somehow.

"What on earth are you going to use that for?" Emily asked Mark.

"Don't know. Hunting perhaps," he said.

"For hunting you'd need a rifle first," she said.

"I would have gotten one, but they didn't have any rifles," Mark replied.

Henry stood by the kitchen door and put down the container. Emily turned and looked at him. "Where's Ollie?" she asked.

Henry shrugged. He hadn't seen him since the morning.

"He said he was going to be with you," Emily said.

"He's not," Henry replied.

Emily checked upstairs, but Ollie wasn't there, so she ran into the yard, calling his name. But the only reply she got was from the raven on the barn roof.

They searched the barn and the sheep sheds, the church and the smithy, but Ollie was nowhere to be found. Emily was becoming hysterical.

"He's your little brother," she cried at Henry. "You should have looked after him!"

The reverend tried to calm her down, but she pushed him away and set out at a run to the edge of the field, shouting Ollie's name.

The raven spread its wings and glided overhead. Henry followed it with his eyes and saw it fly toward the Gallows. It perched upon the higher boulder, sharpening its beak on the rock. Then Henry noticed a flock of seagulls circling high in the air above the two boulders.

At once he realized what had happened.

He limped across the yard as fast as he could, kicking up the gravel as he went, suddenly in a panic, suddenly full of guilt. Was it his fault? Was he to blame if Ollie had come to harm? He had warned him; he had told him it was forbidden, that it was dangerous. Had Ollie followed Spine Break Path, to right all the wrongs that thieves and murderers and all the little children had suffered in ages past?

As Henry reached the path he was almost running. He stumbled and fell and hit his head on a sharp rock, but he jumped up immediately and kept on going. He heard the shouting of the others behind him, calling for Ollie, but his heart was thumping loudly in his chest, the noise of his heavy breathing filling his ears.

The sun hung low in the cloudy sky, the evening breeze growing stronger and colder. The deep rumbling of the ocean below the sea cliffs was threatening; the surf hissed angrily, accusing him: *Your fault. Your fault. Your fault.*

The gulls were circling above the pitch-black crevasse by the Gallows, the deep hole where Henry had once seen the tiny bones. He threw himself down at the edge, searching the pit with his eyes in the growing dusk. Soon it would be too dark to see anything down there.

Ollie seemed so tiny and fragile, lying there facedown at the bottom of the dark pit, his arms spread out as if he were embracing the cold black rocks. One of his moccasins had fallen off his foot, and it struck Henry how strange it was to see his toes, so white and small against the rubble of black lava rock.

The raven croaked angrily upon the boulder, fluttering its wings, frustrated to see the humans coming closer to take the feast away.

Mark and John stumbled over the green moss toward the edge and stopped beside Henry.

"How do we get down there?" Mark said, breathing hard.

Henry shook his head. "We can't," he said.

Suddenly Mark gasped and ran behind the boulders.

"The boat! We've got to hide the boat," he hissed.

John turned around and ran back up Spine Break Path toward Emily and the reverend, but Mark began tearing up the moss, hurriedly trying to cover the white hull of the boat. Henry lay still, looking down at the body at the bottom of the crevasse. It was his little brother. And he had failed to protect him.

The search-and-rescue team was crowded around the crevasse, dressed in orange jackets, with flashlights on their helmets. They had put up big lamps, which flooded the pit with pure white light, and were fastening a line at the edge so two of them could climb down along with a doctor and a stretcher. An ambulance waited in the yard, its blue lights turning in circles on its roof, cutting through the dark evening fog like two laser swords. The ambulance would take Ollie to the city, either to a hospital or a morgue, nobody knew for certain.

Emily had stopped crying. Now she knelt on the edge, wrapped in a warm woolen blanket, the reverend kneeling by her side, his arm around her shoulders. Her hair was drenched from the fog, but she looked indifferent. Her face was hard and cold, and her eyes were fixed on the small body in the pit, illuminated by the strong white floodlights.

When the two men and the doctor finally reached the bottom, Emily stood up and the blanket fell from her shoulders. The doctor examined Ollie quickly, and the two men from the rescue team moved him carefully onto the stretcher. The men on the edge began to pull the stretcher upward, and Emily hid her face in her hands.

The doctor put an oxygen mask on Ollie, and four men carried the stretcher along the path toward the ambulance. As they pushed the stretcher inside, Emily went in and sat by Ollie's side, next to the doctor. Reverend Oswald stood in the yard, looking at her, holding the rain-soaked woolen blanket in his arms. She didn't look up; she saw no one but Ollie. Then someone slammed the doors and the ambulance drove off at full speed. Henry saw the blue lights flashing for a moment on the grave faces of Mark, John, and the reverend. And for a long time the wailing of the siren could be heard through the thin night air, until eventually complete silence took over.

23.

A Journey to Freedom

If there ever had been a real reason to say a prayer at breakfast it should have been now, but the reverend was silent and looking very tired. None of them had slept much. They had all been sitting in the living room, waiting for a phone call from Emily. The boys had dozed off where they sat, but Henry and the reverend had stayed up most of the night, silent, waiting.

It was late in the morning now, closer to lunch than breakfast. The three of them sat at the table while the reverend made some porridge. He put it in a bowl and placed it on the table with a jug full of milk. He didn't sit down to join them; he just stood there, staring at the floor, lost in his thoughts.

The silence was broken when the phone rang, the sound filling every room in the house, loud and demanding. The reverend went to his office and answered it. When he came back his face was even paler than before.

"He's still unconscious," he said. "The doctors are not very optimistic, I'm afraid."

Henry felt a sudden chill go through his heart. The other two lowered their heads.

"I'm going to the hospital to be with Emily. I will have to trust you all until I come back tomorrow morning."

Henry glanced at Mark and knew at once what he was thinking.

The reverend continued. "Tomorrow I'm expecting the whole countryside for the first mass in the new church. Perhaps the Lord will grant us a miracle. We should pray for Ollie and not give in to despair. The Lord works in mysterious ways sometimes, and we don't always know what his plans are; we'll just have to hope for the best, won't we?"

The reverend looked at the boys' glum faces. "You know where everything is," he finally said, "and I'm sure you'll manage to cook something for yourselves tonight."

When the yellow Volvo had disappeared up the road, it was time to prepare for the voyage. Mark gathered tin cans from the pantry and told John to fetch some meat from the freezer. But Henry had to milk the cows. They wouldn't be leaving until the low tide that evening anyway.

The cows chewed on the hay, happily purring. The spark had returned to their eyes: maybe the summer hadn't just been a dream in the winter darkness, but a reality that would possibly repeat itself before too long.

As Henry scraped the dung canal, he had an eerie feeling that Ollie was sitting up on Noah's fence, making his way through one of his books. But when he turned around there was no one there.

Henry worked slowly, leaning his dizzy head against Brandy's soft belly while pulling at her teats, the milk streaming white and warm into the bucket with that familiar sound. His thoughts fluttered about in his mind with great speed, like screeching birds, inches from colliding into one another. Emily's angry accusation about him not having looked after his brother; then his own justification, a whining voice in his head: *I warned him it was dangerous. I told him it was forbidden.* Then Ollie chanting poetry rushed forward in his mind, his silly rhymes, his serious voice saying, "It's important to spread poems over all the places where something bad has happened." Then the dark voice of the roaring ocean followed: *Your fault. Your fault. Your fault.*

He had to get away; he couldn't stay here any longer, knowing that he was to blame. Emily would never forgive him either. Nothing would ever be the same again. He felt the punch on the inside: the fist of the anxiety troll clutching at his heart. They would sail out on the vast ocean, row their little boat in the path of a huge freighter. He would throw the rope with the iron hook and catch the ladder, which Mark had assured him was welded onto the side of the boat. Having climbed on board and hidden in one of the large containers, they would be on their way to Spain, where the sun always shone and the weather was nice and warm, just like in the picture that hung on the wall in his room.

As he emptied the last bucket of milk into the container, he glanced at Ollie's books on the windowsill. Ollie wasn't one of the wicked boys. Henry knew that now. Ollie was just a little boy who needed someone to read for him so he could fall asleep at night. That was all he needed. He had thought ill of him, hated him even, but that was just because he had won Emily's heart so easily, so she cared for nothing and no one but him. And now Henry regretted it terribly, because somehow the little boy had found his way to Henry's heart, and he didn't understand how it had happened.

And now Ollie was dying, perhaps already dead.

Henry took a book from the windowsill and looked at the cover. It was a thin book with a drawing of a funny-looking little boy standing on a planet or something. It looked familiar. He suddenly realized it was the very same book that Emily had given to him, the one he had thrown into the ocean so long ago. Now, as if by a miracle, it was back in his hands.

Beads of cold sweat sprang up on his forehead. His legs gave in and he had to sit down by the wall. He sat there for a long time, staring at the cover, unable to move. Suddenly all was quiet in his head.

The lava field was lined with silver under the moon as they eased the boat over the edge and slowly lowered it down the cliffs. The clouds were black against the purple night sky, but dense clusters on the horizon cast a dark shadow on the ocean far away.

The air was cold, almost freezing, as if the promise of spring had been an illusion or a lie, and winter still ruled the world.

The boat seemed rather small, sitting on the sand below. Mark carried a backpack on his shoulders crammed with stolen food from the kitchen. John carried a wooden box with bottles of milk and water. The chain rattled uncomfortably loudly in the stillness of the night as they eased their way down the cliff wall toward the bank.

The sighs from the undercurrent suggested that it was gradually growing stronger. The waves moved farther out, hesitated a little longer each time, and then fell back with increasing force. The tide was coming in, and they had to hurry.

John climbed on board, and Henry handed him the backpack. He noticed that a large iron hook had been tied securely to a long rope and now lay wound up by the gunwale. John sat down at the back and took a deep breath. The moon was above him, and two stars shone between the clouds: two candles, lit for their journey.

"You go on board," Mark said. "I'll push the boat."

Henry shook his head. "You go," he said.

Mark looked him in the eyes for a second, and then he climbed on board.

Henry leaned forward to push the boat, but Mark grabbed his arm and stopped him.

"Aren't you coming?" he whispered.

The few words that had been exchanged between them that night had been whispered. It was a tense night filled with unspoken anxiety. For a long time now, Henry had had the feeling that this was Mark and John's journey. He'd never been completely convinced that he had really been a part of the plan in the first place, even though Mark had spoken as if it was all settled. Somehow, he had suspected that when the time came, he wouldn't be welcomed on board.

But Mark held his arm so tightly and looked so intensely into his eyes that he hesitated for a moment. Then he shook his head.

"No," he said.

"But your freedom?" Mark said.

"I'm free enough," Henry replied.

"There's nothing for you here," Mark whispered.

Henry hesitated for a moment, trying to find a simple reply, for his real reasons were far too complicated to put in words.

"The cows," Henry said. "I can't leave them."

Mark let go of his arm and sighed. Perhaps he understood, but maybe he was just glad to be rid of him. It was difficult to tell. Henry leaned forward and pushed the boat into the water. Mark raised his hand, and the moon lit up his pale face.

"I'll send you a postcard from Spain, Henry. I promise," he said, and Henry thought he saw a little smile play on his lips.

The boat glided gently from the bank and the keel cut a soft line on the surface. Henry watched the boat move past the wreck, and the undercurrent sighed deeply inside it. Mark hit the water with the oars and rowed steadily toward the open sea, while John raised his hand in a final farewell. Henry turned and climbed the steep path all the way up the edge of the cliff.

He stood there for a long time, like a troll turned to stone, on the edge of the cliff with his clubfoot between the rocks. He peered into the fog that had swallowed the boat, tilted his head, and listened. But all he heard was the gush of the breeze and the slapping surf far below; the air wove between his fingers, a salty spray gently stroked his face. For a moment he thought he heard the faint sound of a harmonica playing a joyful tune, but maybe it was just his imagination.

It had been a desperate plan from the beginning, an insane idea, but who knew; perhaps God would look after them. Perhaps he would work a miracle on their behalf. Maybe Henry didn't have to worry about them anymore; they would be safe now, one way or the other, in that unknown place where dreams came true.

Day was breaking on the eastern sky; the fog dissolved and the birds tumbled off the cliffs and glided over the endless ocean that spread out as far as the eye could see. The bank of dark clouds on the horizon had moved closer; most likely the tempest would reach land tonight.

Henry did as the reverend had asked before leaving yesterday; he moved the chairs from the garage to the new church and arranged them in rows on each side. Then he carried the small organ and placed it beside the altar. Henry had spent the morning alone, getting everything ready for the mass.

He heard the yellow Volvo drive into the yard and saw the reverend disappear into the house. Henry sat down in the church, waiting, but the reverend didn't come.

The crucifix from the garage hung on the wall above the altar. Below it was an electric heater. The cord came in through an open window and stretched all the way across the lava field, right up to the house and into the hall, where it had been connected to a socket.

When Henry heard the cars coming down the road and into the yard, he stood up and walked toward the Cairn of Christ. The Brute was the first one to arrive, in his red pickup. He didn't greet Henry, but Henry didn't mind. He remembered how his fists had crunched the Brute's face, right before someone had hit him on the head, saving the Brute from a messy death.

More cars drove into the yard and a joyful peal rang out from the proud belfry, reverberating in the crisp air. The people from the countryside followed the crooked path toward the church on the knoll.

The Brute was ringing the bell, bidding everyone welcome, saying the reverend would be there in a minute. A handful of men from the city, dressed in smart suits, stepped out of a small bus, looked around with curious smiles, and headed toward the church. Some of them gave Henry a polite nod.

The farmers strode past him, freshly shaven, with tightly knotted ties pressing against their throats, and their wives were all dressed up as well. But none of them greeted him. Henry heard some of them making jokes about the reverend and his wife, their cattle, the boys. They probably felt pretty fancy in their Sunday clothes, but Henry thought they looked stupid and awkward. They were mean-looking people with mockery in their eyes, malicious grins on their ugly faces, the women giggling like hens.

So these were the people on whose behalf Reverend Oswald had sacrificed the sheep, made the little ones toil, and murdered Noah? He had done all that to raise money for a church for them? These were the people the reverend wanted to impress, the people he wanted to save so they could go to heaven? Who would want to go to heaven if these people were there?

Henry spat on the ground as a group passed by.

The breeze blew gently against his cheeks and the sky was clear.

The many voices of spring could be heard from the lava field, mixed with the low rumble of the surf. Soon the grass would turn green by the roadside and the bushes would sprout leaves in the lava. It wouldn't be long until he untied Old Red and let her lead the group to pasture. And there was no doubt he would be allowed to drive the tractor this summer.

Now all the guests had entered the church and taken their seats, but Reverend Oswald was nowhere to be seen. Henry sat still by the cairn and waited.

A sudden chirp caught his attention; the little gray bird with the long black tail had arrived. It sat upon the white cross on top of the cairn, chirping sweetly, as if bidding Henry good morning. Then it vanished into the sky.

After a long while, the church door opened. The Brute stepped out and looked around him. He strode up to the house, banged the door with his fist, and peered through the windows. But no one came. He looked back toward the church, shrugged, and shook his head. A moment later the guests came out of the church and walked toward their cars, fuming with anger, some of them cursing.

They glanced angrily at Henry for a second, but no one spoke to him. The freshly shaven farmers didn't look so happy anymore and their dolled-up wives didn't either. The men in the suits stepped into their bus with angry frowns and drove away. Gravel shot out from under the wheels as the cars sped out of the yard, one after the other.

The breeze blew the dust gently toward the empty church on the knoll that stood proudly on its solid foundation. There were three white windows on each side and a white cross on the belfry; the corrugated iron roof was glowing like silver. The reverend's dream had finally come true. But there was no one rejoicing.

24.

Reading for Ollie

Reverend Oswald was in the Boiler Room.

He was lying on the bed, fully clothed, but sleeping. On the floor were a suitcase and three pairs of shoes in a plastic bag. Henry poked his shoulder several times before the reverend opened his eyes and turned around.

"Are they gone?" he whispered.

Henry nodded. The reverend sat up in bed and asked Henry to take a seat on a chair. Henry sat down and waited while the reverend rubbed his eyes and cleared his throat several times. Then he put on his glasses, but he didn't look at Henry while he talked, he gazed through the open door, into the empty hall.

"I couldn't go through with it, not after what has happened," he said with a heavy sigh. "What should I be preaching, anyway?" he said, and lowered his head.

Henry had no answer to that. He only wanted to know about Ollie, and if Emily was coming back.

"He's still unconscious," the reverend said, as if he had read Henry's thoughts. "And if he should die, Emily is not coming back."

"Never?" Henry said.

"Not to live with me, anyway," the reverend replied dryly, rubbing his forehead. "That's why I'm packing; that's why I'm leaving."

He sighed and glanced at Henry for a while, maybe wondering if he could open his heart to him, perhaps wondering if Henry could understand anything at all. Maybe Oswald just needed a friend, Henry thought.

"She always wanted a child of her own, you know," the reverend said. "But I had this idea about a home for troubled boys on a farm in the countryside." He grinned and continued, "It was my project, something that mattered to me, and she loved the idea, and the countryside as well. But somehow it all failed. Why did it fail, Henry? Where did I go wrong?"

Henry clasped his hands in his lap and knew that the reverend wasn't really asking him a question. He was just thinking out loud, like people did, sitting with a trusted friend. And at this moment Henry seemed to be the only one left for the reverend.

"One night I walked up the stairs. I saw her sleeping in our bed, and the little boy was sleeping beside her. She had her arm around him, as if to protect him, her slow breath gently stirring his blond hair.

"Then I realized that I had failed her, for she didn't need me anymore. One is never so lonely as when one's kindness is no longer needed."

The reverend took off his glasses and wiped his eyes with his fingers. Then he continued.

"I was a young boy once, you know, with nightmares of my own. All I ever wanted was to protect others from their nightmares. I had a stepfather, you see. He was the monster of my nightmares. He tried to make me a man by telling me over and over again that I was worthless. He said that to toughen me up, you see," the reverend said in a dull voice. Then he drew his breath deeply and let out a tired sigh.

"But I was slow to learn. And I was never tough, so it was difficult not to cry.

"When the humiliation hurt too much, I made myself disappear into another world, where I alone was in control. A world where all my dreams came true, a world full of miracles, happiness, and harmony."

He turned to Henry with a weak smile on his lips.

"And that is my biggest failure, I guess. Believing that absolute control would make everything all right."

He fell silent for a while, hunched forward as if he was about to fall on the floor. Then he put his glasses back on and cleared his throat. He sat up straight and clasped his hands.

"I'm sorry I sold the bull for slaughter, Henry. I'm really sorry for what I made you go through. I hope you can find it in your heart to forgive me, son."

Then he stood up and grabbed the plastic bag with his shoes from the floor. Henry stood up as well and without thinking he grabbed the handle of the suitcase. The reverend looked at him and smiled warmly.

"Thank you, Henry."

Henry stood by the Cairn of Christ as the yellow Volvo

disappeared up the road. The dark-purple mass of clouds was looming overhead. Soon it would be raining hard. He watched the clouds roll across the sky, blocking out the sun, heading toward the land. When the first drops fell on the gravel around him, Henry stood up and limped over to the cowshed. He still had to milk the cows, but he wondered what he should do with the milk, now that there was no Ollie to drink it and no Emily to make butter. After milking, he poured the milk into the container as usual and listened to the wind slashing the rain on the corrugated iron roof. He thought about John and Mark in the small boat somewhere out on the vast ocean, hoping they were safe. But they were in the hands of God now. One way or the other they'd be all right. There was nothing Henry could do about that now.

The wind squeezed through a crack in the window, stirring the paperback cover on Ollie's book, as if it wanted to leaf through the pages. Somewhere in some hospital Ollie lay under a duvet. Henry wondered if there were people who had time to read for little children in hospitals.

He limped across the lava field, in the soaking rain, with Ollie's book in one hand, his other hand clenched into a tight fist. The rain hammered the corrugated iron on the small church and poured like a waterfall off the edge of the roof.

He opened the door and stepped inside.

The noise was almost deafening in there and seemed to come from every direction; like a thousand whispering voices one moment, and a thousand screaming voices the next, making him jump. On the floor, the heads of the nails were like silver coins thrust into the floorboards. Raindrops fell from the ceiling, here and there, hitting the floor with a loud snapping sound, like when a thin twig is broken in two.

Henry sat down at the altar, wiped the water off his face with both hands, and stared straight ahead. The storm shook the church and the rain beat the iron like a hundred hammers. Suddenly someone shouted his name. He gave a start, but it was just the storm, pounding the roof. His heart was racing, for he was terrified, not because of the noise and the weather, but because he had made up his mind.

He grabbed the book, put it on his knees, and wiped the raindrops off the cover with his sleeve. Then he opened it to page one and stared at the letters for a long time. At first they were all one big jumble before his eyes, and he felt a pain in his stomach. But then he began to read in a low, hesitant voice that sounded rusty and coarse. It wasn't a long story, but it took him a long time to stutter through it all. He didn't give up, he forced himself, clenching his fists now and then, ripping the words off the page, one by one, and releasing them through his mouth. When he had finally mumbled through the whole book, all the way to the end, he looked up, breathing heavily, red in the face. The howling storm continued to pound the roof, and the rain had turned to hail. Even if he shouted at the top of his voice, there was no chance of anyone hearing him.

He leafed back to page one and started again.

As he wrestled with the words and sentences, he forgot himself and fell silent while he examined the illustrations before continuing to the very end. Then he went back to the beginning and started again. Little by little, he began to recognize the words and remember them. His reading became less hesitant and he almost completely lost his stutter.

It was a story about a little prince, a pilot, a rose, and a sheep. And the prince meets a fox who tells him the secret of friendship: "It is only with the heart that one can see rightly; what is essential is invisible to the eye."

Henry no longer felt his body and had stopped hearing the weather. All his emotions were being channeled through his voice and the words that streamed out of him. He was reading for Ollie.

The church trembled and the hail hammered the roof, but his words glided in the air, joyful and bright like the birds at the cliffs. They floated freely around one another without colliding and the wind carried them high up into heaven.

He woke up in the middle of the night, fully dressed in his bed.

The rain had stopped, a light breeze whispered on the roof, and the cows sighed in their stalls. Suddenly he felt strange and uncomfortable in there, surrounded by the gray walls, the smell from the barn, the breathing of the cows. His chest felt heavy, so he stood up and limped outside.

The air was cool and clean, and the moss looked like silver in the light of the moon. Two black clouds hung quite still in the purple sky, like shreds of old cloth.

When he reached the cliffs, he sat down on the edge. He could hardly hear the gentle waves caressing the rocks far below. Silk ribbons of moonlight moved side by side on the still ocean.

Henry knew that crying didn't change anything; his mother had taught him that. And he hadn't cried in a long time. He had just been angry, balling his fists up tightly. But now his fists lay open in his lap, and the silk ribbons of the ocean untangled before his eyes and turned into a misty haze. Warm teardrops fell into his palms. He didn't make a sound except for the occasional gasp for air. It came so easily. He knew that crying wouldn't change anything, so what harm could it do now? It wouldn't bring back what he had lost, but it couldn't take anything more away from him either.

25.

A Whole Leg of Lamb

Henry could do nothing but wait, so he went to the house to find something to eat.

Somehow the house had no soul anymore. It was abandoned and silent. The kitchen was a mess: dirty plates in the sink, a pot of cold porridge on the stove, a bottle half full of milk turned sour. In the living room a stack of books on the floor; beside it a cup of cold coffee and a plate with a stale sandwich. Henry wondered if he should turn on the television and find something to watch. But he didn't want to disturb the silence in the house.

He sat for a long time on the chair by the cold stove, feeling hungry.

Finally he found a leg of lamb in the fridge and decided to cook it. He put it in the oven and took some time to figure out how to turn up the heat. He found some potatoes and carrots in a cupboard and put them in a pot on the stove.

Then he moved the chair and sat in front of the oven, watching the leg of lamb cook. He cried a little and felt sorry for himself. It was a relief; it actually felt good.

When the meat was thoroughly cooked he put it on a large

plate along with the potatoes and the carrots. Then he ate his fill and cried a little more, feeling very miserable and lonely. But after a while he didn't feel that bad anymore.

He went to bed early, hoping that the morning would bring him some news of Emily. But nobody came and nothing happened.

There was little else he could do but carry on with his routine and wait for someone to arrive. Occasionally he heard the distant foghorn of a freighter echo across the vast ocean. Then he thought about Mark and John and imagined them sitting on some beach in Spain, enjoying the sun. Maybe everything had worked out according to plan; hopefully they had found freedom, one way or the other.

In the evening he read Ollie's book again, over and over, until he fell asleep. He read it out loud and in silence too. He even included the page numbers, not missing a thing. He knew the story by heart now, every single page, every single word. And each time he began reading, he imagined that Ollie was by his side, listening. Why hadn't he had the courage to read for Ollie when he'd had the chance?

Three days went by.

He had cooked two legs of lamb, boiled some fish he'd found in the freezer, and finished the coffee and the porridge. He spent a whole evening cleaning the kitchen, washing the plates and the forks and the knives, the pots and the pans, and finished by scrubbing the floor, the way Emily had always done.

During the day, Henry sat by the Cairn of Christ, watching for some movement up on the road.

The moss and heather gave off a thick spicy scent, and the sweet warmth of the bright sun caressed his cheeks. He heard the deep rumbling of the surf down by the cliffs. It was the kind of morning where the birds would hurl themselves into the void and rise high in the air, carried on the back of the strong breeze.

The tiny gray bird leaped around on the cairn, waving its long black tail, holding a thin straw in its tiny beak. It had found a safe home for its little ones in between the rocks of the Cairn of Christ. Henry couldn't help but smile. At least someone would raise their children in the shelter of the Savior. Boy and bird pondered each other for a moment. Then the bird flew up and disappeared.

Henry heard the rumble of an engine. He rose to his feet as he saw the bus turn toward the farm. There was a cloud of brown dust as the bus stopped with a heavy sigh.

Henry felt his throat tighten as he watched Emily step out. His heart was beating fast and everything he had felt rushed through him in an instant. It didn't help to clench his jaw now or his fists. This time, he just had to let go. He covered his face with his large hands, pressing his thick fingers into his forehead, trembling from grief, crying hard.

He stood like that, utterly helpless, until he felt her gentle arms embrace him tightly. She held him for a long time, giving him all the time he needed to empty his heart of all his loneliness and fear, shivering like a lost child having so unexpectedly found the loving embrace of his mother again.

"We're back, Henry," she whispered in his ear. "And everything will be all right now."

Henry wiped his face and looked at her, not believing.

Standing beside her, smiling brightly, was his little brother.

"I'm here," Ollie said.

Epilogue

Henry's Last Letter

Dear Ollie,

This will be a short letter and my last one too, and that's a promise.

I think I've written everything I wanted to tell you about, and I'm also getting real tired of writing. It's very hard work. But there was much that I'd always wanted to tell you. And now I have.

Now I just look forward to riding my horse down the valley, all the way to the beach. Do you remember the golden sand? That's my favorite route, riding along the beach, with the surf on my left and the green fields on my right.

I still remember our first morning here at the new farm. You were so tired that you slept like a log. But I couldn't wait to go out and look at the green mountains and the broad river, winding its way through the fields toward the ocean at the mouth of the valley. Everything was so different from the old place. And so much better.

I like to imagine that John and Mark made it to Spain, but I doubt it. Their parents sued the reverend, and he got a long sentence. The papers called him a murderer, because neither the boat nor the boys were ever found again. I felt bad for a very long time. After all, it was me who showed them the boat in the first place. And it was me who pushed the boat into the water. But I was just a kid.

I almost went with them that night, you know. And maybe that would have been the end of my story. Then I never would have known happiness. Imagine that. One simple decision is all you need to change your life forever. Like deciding to stay or to go; to say yes or no, turn right or left.

If you hadn't arrived at the reverend's little farm in hell, with your books and your mouth full of words, I could have been lost at sea with John and Mark. You and your funny poems, especially the one about the sun, somehow made me change my mind that night. I can't describe how or why. I don't know the words for that. But I did, and so I didn't perish. Instead I moved to this place with you and Emily, a place pretty close to heaven, if you ask me.

We have fifty sheep now, and as you know they're Emily's joy, especially in the lambing season. I've got twelve cows, a brand-new milking machine, and a fine strong bull. Last year I bought another horse, so now there's one for you when you come back.

When will you come back to visit?

Last Christmas you were in Scotland, and the year before somewhere in France. I know you're busy and all, but your home is here.

Ever since you left I've set the table for three on all your birthdays, and filled your glass with milk. All those years you've been away I've also finished your slice of birthday cake. And every Christmas I've put your plate on the living-room table where you used to sit at dinner. Maybe it sounds funny, but this makes me feel that you are back home with us. Like you never really left.

I've read your books about the great kings of old times. It's really strange, but those are the only books I read that make me fall asleep almost instantly. I guess you could say I'm not that interested in history. But that's not the reason; when I read your words I can hear your voice reading to me.

And then you're not so far away anymore.

Maybe you're imagining that I miss you terribly, Ollie, and perhaps you're feeling really bad about that. But you shouldn't. You must believe me when I say I don't miss you at all. It's true. The reason is that, instead of missing you, I just really look forward to the day you'll come back.

I hope you haven't forgotten how the farm looks or where to get off the bus. Just so you won't get lost, I can tell you that the walking distance from the main road up to the farm is exactly three verses from the "Poem of the Sun."

Your brother, Henry